CONSPIRACY 365

BOOK TWO: FEBRUARY

GABRIELLE LORD

Hodder
Children's
Books

A division of Hachette Children's Books

Note: This story is set in Australia, where February is a summer month

To Hélène, Jessica and Sam

PREVIOUSLY...

31 DECEMBER
I'm chased by a madman, who tells me my dad
was murdered, and that I will be too if I don't
hide out until midnight, next December 31st.
365 days . . .

1 JANUARY
I somehow survive a boating accident during a
violent storm in shark-infested waters.

2 JANUARY
Our house gets broken into and trashed.

9 JANUARY
Some woman's called me claiming to have information on my dad. But before we meet I'm
kidnapped and interrogated by a group of
criminals.

10 JANUARY

After narrowly escaping my captors, my uncle and little sister are brutally attacked. Rafe is recovering in hospital and Gabbi's on life support. *My* face is on the news as the attacker! The police are after me now, too! I've got no choice but to run.

13 JANUARY

I'm hiding out in a St Johns Street dump, trying to make sense of the crazy drawings Dad did just before he died, and trying to figure out a way to clear my name.

31 JANUARY

I'm grabbed off the street by another criminal gang, this time led by the infamous Vulkan Sligo. When he realises I have no information to give him, he traps me in a fast-filling underground oil tank . . . and leaves me there to drown . . .

1 FEBRUARY

334 days to go . . .

Car yard

12:00 am

The stinking sump oil gushed out of the pipe on my right, relentlessly filling the underground tank I was trapped in. I struggled to hold my mouth above the rising tide as I bashed my slippery fists on the manhole cover at my head. It was useless. It wouldn't budge.

Car wheels screeched and sped away in the distance, reminding me that I was completely alone. Left to die.

12:03 am

No matter how hard I tried to move around in the thick, glue-like oil, I couldn't stop it from climbing my face. My mouth was almost completely covered. I shut it tight. I desperately pushed my head back and forced my nostrils—

my last chance at life—up and away from the surface that was swallowing me whole.

You've got to slow down your breathing, I told myself. I knew it would be certain death if my nose started sucking up the oil. The powerful, caustic fumes burned through my insides like acid. My head spun, and fear made me breathe faster and harder.

My own voice, from moments ago, played back in my mind . . . *Red hair. Purple sunglasses.* But I'd never even seen the woman who'd abducted me the first time, so what in the world had made me describe her like that to Sligo?!

And, even more puzzling, he seemed to know who I was talking about—he knew someone from the conference that fitted that exact description! What was going on?

I had escaped death at sea, just a month ago, only to find myself facing it again. But there was no possible escape from this.

12:04 am

The oil reached the bottom of my nose. Any moment now and it would block my nostrils entirely . . . I strained my muscles harder, trying to lift my body even just a millimetre higher, but it was impossible; there was nowhere to go.

I started inhaling droplets of oil. *365 days . . .*

the crazy guy's deranged warning from New Year's Eve screamed through my mind, taunting me. I'd only made it through one month—whatever lethal force had cursed my family had finally got to me. A few more seconds and I wouldn't be able to breathe . . . I closed my eyes and hoped it would be quick.

12:05 am

I was so intensely focused on letting myself die calmly that I didn't hear the exact moment the gushing stopped. But, for some reason, it *had* stopped. Somehow, the flow had been turned off!

Some sort of miracle had put an end to the process. What had happened? I was shaking all over. I was almost completely submerged in oil, but I was alive . . .

I opened my eyes, still straining to keep my nostrils higher than the level of the oil, and listened . . .

Nothing.

I slowly pulled up my arm, trying to avoid making a wave that would swamp my face, and thumped on the cover above me.

I pushed myself closer into the corner, hoping to exert more pressure. But it was a waste of energy. Yeah, the oil might have stopped, but I was just as hopelessly trapped as I was before.

12:09 am

The relief I'd felt a moment ago started turning into horror. I was stupid to think that the end of the gushing oil meant I'd survived, and that someone had come to my rescue; I was no closer to making it unless I got out.

My mind raced. Maybe it would have been better for the tank to fill completely, so that I could have at least drowned quickly. Now I was going to be stuck in the darkness of the tank and die of asphyxiation or, worse, slowly and painfully from thirst!

I strained to listen for a sign of hope outside my oil-filled tomb, but all I could hear in the silence was the beating of my blood against my eardrums—the thumping of my fighting heart.

How was I going to get out of this?

12:18 am

'Hey!'

A *voice*?

'You in the tank,' it continued. 'You OK?'

OK? Someone was asking me if I was OK? Was I hearing things? I was so light-headed from fumes and adrenaline that I wasn't sure of anything. I wanted to yell out but there was no way I could open my mouth. I had to make *some* noise, somehow, to let whoever was out there know I was still alive. I was terrified I'd miss my chance—if it even was a chance—and be left there for dead when I was so close to making it.

I took a slow, careful breath through my nose, shut my eyes tight, and thumped at the manhole cover with my fists. Oil splashed all over my face.

I stopped and waited.

I knew I couldn't hold my breath much longer.

Just as I was giving up on hope of air, there was a creaking, grinding noise. Someone was twisting open the cover!

It lifted and soft light fell on the sea of black surrounding me. I hauled myself up the ladder and out of the opening, spitting and gasping. I'd freed my mouth and nostrils from the deadly tide and re-emerged into life.

I coughed and wheezed uncontrollably, madly shaking my oil-soaked head. I clung to the ground while my lower half hung exhausted below me, still in the tank and submerged in oil.

'Who's there?' I finally managed to croak, spitting oil from my lips.

No answer.

'Hello?' I asked again, cautiously looking around.

Was I imagining things? Was this some trick or some sort of mental torture that Vulkan Sligo was inflicting on me?

'Why don't you pull yourself out already? Or do you like hanging out in there?'

There was no mistake, it was a voice. The voice of a girl. I struggled to climb a little higher. My clothes and shoes were heavy and saturated, and my feet skidded, banging my shins hard into the ladder.

Eventually I crawled all the way out of the tank and rolled over onto my back, exhausted.

Something loomed in my vision. I blinked and tried to focus.

Above me stood the girl I'd seen earlier in the office with Sligo; the one with the strange eye make-up and wild hair. She stared down at me with her shadowed, almond-shaped eyes.

'Who are you?' I asked, groggily. 'Did you turn the oil off?'

'Look at you,' she said pointing down at me. 'You look like a swamp monster!'

What?

'Actually, your eyes and forehead are still human. Kind of!' she laughed.

After all I'd been through, this girl was cracking jokes? I started lifting myself to my feet, trying to think of something clever to throw back at her, but instead I slipped and fell, landing heavily on my side.

I sat back up to hear more laughter. The girl was laughing at me again!

'You should see yourself!' she said as I crawled away from the tank. 'Believe me, it's funny!'

I tried to stand up again and this time the girl grabbed my flailing right hand, with a surprisingly strong grip, and steadied me. As I balanced myself so I could stand without her help, one of my greasy trainers skidded out from under me and down again I crashed.

The girl was still gripping my hand, so she came down too and fell awkwardly on top of me. At least that stopped her laughing.

She scrambled to her feet, and scrunched up her face in disgust. Her hands and clothes were covered in oil too.

'Look what you've done!' she yelled.

'Just like a swamp monster,' I jeered. 'You should see *your*self!'

She looked down, unsuccessfully trying to rub the black muck off.

'I've gotta get this off me,' she said, turning and running towards a building behind the office where I'd been interrogated. I followed, squelching after her.

12:38 am

We were in some sort of laundry. The girl was washing her face over a big steel tub. A cracked mirror hung above the basin I was standing in front of and I was shocked to see my reflection: the whites of my eyes stared out of a messy black head, and oil crawled down my face in gluey streams and dripped onto the floor.

My heart rate started to slow down a little. I was alive, and I was out.

'You're not going to get very far looking like that,' she warned, peering up at me with dark, smudged eyes. 'You'd better be quick if you want to clean up, they'll be back soon to fish your body out of the tank, and if they find you here instead of there, you're not the only one that'll be in trouble.'

She rushed around and kept looking past me towards the door. Although she had a pretty face, her eyes were cold and unsmiling. But, for some reason, she'd stuck around to save my life.

'OK,' I said, 'but I have to grab my backpack, first.'

'I've already helped enough. I'm getting out of here the second I've cleaned up. You're on your own.'

I quickly washed some of the oil off my face. I knew I didn't have long to get the answers I needed but surely this stranger could tell me something . . .

'What's your story?' I asked her. 'What are you doing with Vulkan Sligo, and why did you help me?'

She wiped her face hurriedly with a towel. 'You want to know why I helped you?' she asked. Clearly she didn't want to answer the first part of my question.

'I helped because . . . I liked your piercings,' she said.

'You saved my life because of my *studs*?' I quickly felt around to see if my fake studs were even still there. And then I remembered Gabbi's Celtic ring and felt frantically for it on my hand. Relieved, I found it clinging on tight.

'You got a problem with that?' she threatened. 'What does it matter, anyway? You're alive, aren't ya? Isn't that enough?'

This girl was unbelievable.

'You'd better hurry up if you want to *stay* alive,' she added. 'I'm serious, Sligo will be back any minute, and if he sees me—' she paused and slung her bag over her shoulder, 'he'll know it was me who got you out. We can't let that happen. He can't even find out that I *knew* you were in the tank.'

'I get it,' I said. She didn't need to warn me.

I knew all about danger. Sligo had just left me to drown. I knew what he was capable of. 'But first we need to get back into the office to grab my bag.'

The girl brushed down her damp skirt. '*We?* I'm sorry, but like I just said, I don't have time. I don't want to end up in the oil tank like you. I don't think I'd have anyone coming to *my* rescue.'

She grabbed her scarf from the basin and headed for the door.

'Wait! Who are you? Why did you help me?'

She pushed past me on her way out, slowing briefly at the doorway. 'Look, I can wait a few minutes for you down the road. But it's too dangerous for me to hang around here any longer. If you do get away before Sligo comes back, don't go through the main entrance; use the small gate in the back corner of the car yard.' She looked at her watch then started running, turning briefly to yell back, 'I'm only waiting a few minutes, got it?'

'But my bag!' I shouted. 'The office is locked!'

Her voice drifted back. 'There's a spare key on top of the window frame.'

I ran around to the stairs in front of the office, leaving dark, wet footprints behind me. I hurried to the verandah and stretched up, feeling along the top of the window frame to my right.

Nothing.

There was the sound of an approaching car. It had to be Sligo or his thugs coming back to collect my body.

I launched up towards the top of the left-hand window frame and my scrabbling fingers finally lucked onto a key. I almost dropped it—I was still slipping everywhere—but somehow I managed to unlock the door. My backpack was exactly where I'd seen it last—shoved in the bin. I lunged and snatched it, and in one move was outside again.

I couldn't hear the car any more. The yard looked deserted. Maybe it hadn't been Sligo coming back after all.

I kicked off my oil-drenched jeans and pulled on another pair from my bag, struggling to drag them over my wet skin. I threw on my hoodie and began running, hoping this wasn't the kind of place that had bloodthirsty dogs prowling around.

A powerful, automatic light suddenly flooded the area. I swung around and realised that I was standing, startled stiff, in headlights! The car was right there behind me!

I started running again. Brilliant headlights shifted and followed me as the car drove further into the yard.

Two men jumped out and came after me on foot. I bolted away, counting on finding the gate that the girl had told me to use. I kept low as I scrambled over rusty car parts, engines and other bits of machinery until finally I spotted the gate in the wire fence.

I broke cover and made a run for it.

1:01 am

The thugs shouted and thundered behind me. I put my head down and drove my legs as hard as I could.

When I'd made it a few hundred metres from the gate, I slowed down a little, scanning the street for the girl. She suddenly emerged from the bushes.

'Run!' I yelled. 'They're coming!'

Without a word she joined me and we both pounded along the road together, turning up and down streets without even thinking—anything to get as far away as possible from that place. Away from Sligo. Away from the oil tank. Away from danger.

1:23 am

Eventually the sound of our pursuers died away and we stopped running. I leaned heavily against a brick fence, trying to catch my breath. The girl had also stopped and was panting nearby. She looked down at the palms of her hands and I noticed, under the thin stream of street light, that they were red, swollen and blistered. She must have hurt them turning off the oil.

She suddenly looked up and caught me staring at her hands.

'And you haven't even said thanks,' she snapped.

1:25 am

'Believe me,' I pleaded. 'I'm grateful. Thanks . . . I don't even know your name.'

She ignored me and started walking off. She *had* saved my life, so if she wanted silence I'd let her have it. For now.

We loped along together, and I hoped we'd put enough distance between us and the Slug for the time being. I was sweating from the heat of the night and all of that hard running. What a life.

'I know *your* name,' she suddenly said, raising her eyes and shifting her embroidered shoulder bag from one side to the other. 'Everyone in the city knows your name. Sligo certainly does.'

Closer up I could see green-gold flecks in her dark eyes. I also noticed that her wild and wavy hair had little sparkles in it.

'I know,' I said. But what did she mean by that? Sligo didn't seem the sort of guy who'd be interested in a teenage fugitive, so there was only one reason why he'd be after me—somehow, he must have known something about my dad's life-changing discovery. I knew he'd already found out about the angel, a jewel and the riddle. Maybe something had been leaked to him from the conference in Ireland.

1:32 am

We'd stopped again and everything was still and quiet, except for the crickets. I felt like I was shaking all over. It must have been some sort of delayed shock.

We were surrounded by suburban houses; I was sure all the families inside them would have long ago been tucked into bed. I thought of Mum, sleepless in our house, suburbs away, and Gabbi on life support, alone in the hospital. Mum had almost lost our whole family—first Dad, Gabbi in a way, and now me. I wanted my old life back so badly and wished I wasn't this hunted kid, on the run, living in a derelict dump, trying to stay one jump ahead of . . . of everyone.

'I overhear things,' said the girl, suddenly interrupting my thoughts. 'I know you've got something Sligo wants.'

I looked down the long street. 'You know what that is?' I asked. It would be great if this girl had a few real answers for me.

She shook her head and the glitter in her hair flashed. 'Only that it's massive, and that he'll stop at nothing to get it.'

'So I've noticed.'

'But I knew you didn't know anything about it,' she said matter-of-factly. 'You would have told him if you did. Anybody would have . . . over drowning in sump oil.'

Finally something straightforward that I could agree with. 'You seem to know so much about me. It's hardly fair I don't even know your name,' I said, hoping for the straight talk to continue. I was careful—I didn't want to scare her off. I owed her for shutting off the oil pump, and there were so many questions I needed to ask. Not just about Sligo and what he knew about my dad, but about her. She'd helped me—saved my life—but what was she doing with Sligo? I couldn't make her out. She was nothing like the girls I knew from school. But, as strange as she was, she was company, and it felt good to have someone around to talk to . . . someone who wasn't trying to kill me.

'I'll tell you my name when we get there,' she said.

'Get where? I thought we were just getting *away*.'

'Now you're going to help *me*.'

'Is that right? You could have just asked for my help,' I suggested. 'Nobody likes being bossed around, especially not by some nameless girl.'

With one hand on her hip, she stared back at me with intense eyes. 'All right. My name is Winter,' she said. 'Winter Frey. Happy?'

'Fancy name,' I said.

'Fancy suits me,' she replied.

I was trying to think of something funny to say back when a car turned onto the road ahead, about a block away. I didn't wait to see if it was the black Subaru; I just grabbed Winter's hand and hauled her off the footpath and into a bushy driveway. I let go of her, but not before noticing a tiny tattoo of a bird on the inside of her left wrist. She pulled away quickly, protectively folding her arms, and we both huddled down, sneaking glimpses of the car slowly rolling past.

'Sligo's car,' she hissed.

We waited, hidden in the darkness, until we were sure that the car had gone. Winter looked around. 'Let's go.'

1:49 am

My body felt wrecked. My face was swollen from being roughed up, my shins and arms were aching from the struggle in the tank, and my old injury in my right shoulder pinched, making sure I hadn't forgotten it. I kept seeing Winter's bird tattoo in my mind, wondering what she was doing roaming the streets with me—some fugitive kid—in the middle of the night.

'What are you doing with Vulkan Sligo?' I finally asked again. I'd wasted enough time trying to imagine a reason why a girl like that would have anything to do with a guy like him.

Winter turned to me under the shelter of a large tree. I kept my eyes on the street, scanning for any sign of movement.

'You really wanna know?'

'That's what I said.'

'The answer is simple. He's my guardian.'

'Your guardian? What do you mean? Where are your parents?'

Around us the air was suddenly very still and cold.

'You ask too many questions,' she said.

'I'm only after basic information.'

'Get it somewhere else. OK?'

I shrugged.

'And,' she resumed, 'even though he's my guardian, there's no way I'd hang around him unless—'

'Unless what?' I interrupted. 'Is it because you're some kind of outlaw too? Birds of a feather flock together?' I looked again for the tiny bird on her wrist.

She shook her hair and a million tiny sparkles flashed. 'I have my reasons. Very good reasons that I don't have to explain to anyone. And he needs me. Even if only to help him change his image.'

'Change his image? He wants to go straight? Is that what you're trying to tell me?' I couldn't believe what I was hearing. 'He almost *murdered* me a moment ago and now you're telling me he wants to change his image? Too funny!'

'It might sound like a joke to you, but there's one thing you should know about Sligo. He has ambitions. He doesn't like being called a criminal by the media.'

'He *is* a criminal! Forget what the media does or doesn't call him!'

'You've got to understand, he doesn't see it like that. He's desperate to be seen as straight—respectable. That was the whole reason he was interested in you.'

'So interested he wants to drown me? I'm not getting you, Winter.'

'He wanted to use you, somehow, and, well, obviously his plans didn't exactly work out. Look, I don't have to justify anything to you. Just believe me when I tell you that this massive thing he's chasing—the reason for the interrogation—it's all tied up with his pathetic attempt to eventually be . . . respected and admired. That's all there really is to it.'

The Ormond Singularity, I thought. Did it have the power to make the crooked straight?

'Sometimes I suspect he's only using *me*,' Winter continued. 'My family is—was—very wealthy. We owned property from the highlands right down to Dolphin Point. My parents were both very successful and well known . . . in their circles.'

She hesitated and I sensed something like deep sorrow that had been frozen over. 'Sligo used to work for my father . . .' her voice faltered, 'before the accident.'

She stopped speaking.

'The accident?' I asked, cautiously.

'I don't want to talk about it,' she said, cutting me off. Her eyes cooled over again in an instant, and she flashed them in warning at me.

An accident that took both of her parents? I wanted to ask more, but I stopped myself—she'd made it clear that the subject was too painful. She suddenly didn't seem quite so fearless. It was bad enough losing Dad—but I still had Mum. Kind of.

'Answer me something,' she said, interrupting my thoughts.

'Do you always talk like that?' I asked. 'Like you're commanding an army?'

Winter flung her head to one side. 'It's just a simple question. Are you any good at breaking into houses?'

Mansfield Way, Dolphin Point

2:02 am

We'd arrived in front of a huge house which was set back quite a distance from the road. The property was surrounded by bushes and a tall, intimidating, black iron fence. It was number 113, according to the polished brass numbers on the gate. The neighbouring houses were just as huge and daunting, but they were all lined up in perfect unison—polished and proud—unlike this place that seemed a little overgrown and unkempt.

I turned to Winter. 'You want to break into this?' I asked, exhausted. 'No way. You must be out of your mind. It's probably covered in cameras.'

She looked me up and down. 'It's not as secure as it looks,' she said, slipping open the gate with ease. 'See? And anyway, maybe I should have phrased that better. I'm really just visiting a friend.'

'Right,' I said, 'and does your "friend" know you're coming?'

'Well, actually . . . so it's not exactly a visit.'

'So, what is it?'

'It's a—I guess you *can* really only call it a break-in,' she said. 'There's something in there that I have to collect and I'd really *appreciate* it if you joined me.'

That's just great, I thought. Here I was already on the run, having survived a murder attempt, with criminals after me, cops after me, and now this girl wanted me to help her break into a Dolphin Point mansion?

'What's your problem?' she asked icily, as her eyes narrowed. 'I saved your life, remember? And according to the media, you've already attempted murder. Twice. Psycho-teen, they're calling you. What's a little break-in compared with that? If you don't want to help me, I can just ring *my* Sligo, and have his thugs here in five minutes. You can't run very far in five minutes.'

What was with this girl, threatening me?! Had she only saved me so that she could use me? Was she nothing but a user like Sligo?

'Anyway,' she said, quickly sensing my changing mood, 'it's not a robbery.' She pulled me through the gate after her. 'The girl who's living here has something important that belonged to my mum. I just need to collect what's mine.'

'And why doesn't your mum ask for it back?' I asked, knowing it was sure to upset her. But as soon as the words came out of my mouth, I wished I could have taken them back.

Winter looked away, but not before I'd recognised the sharp blow of grief that hit her face. She grabbed my hoodie and wrenched me down behind a line of thick bushes. 'My mum can't ask for anything,' she whispered firmly in my ear. 'My mum's dead.'

I pulled away from her grip.

'I'm sorry,' I whispered.

Winter shrugged.

'I shouldn't have said that . . . I know how you feel,' I offered.

Winter glared at me. 'You *know*? What would *you* know about it! You're just some stiff suburban school kid who's suddenly stumbled into some trouble. You think you're an expert now?! Ha!'

'Look,' I said, 'keep it down. Do you want us to get caught out here already?' I felt no need whatsoever to explain myself to her.

I could see her trying to work out what to say. Her eyes narrowed as she spoke, 'Anyway,' she said, 'the guy that lives here—the boyfriend—works as a bodyguard for Murray Durham—'

'Murray Durham?!' I cut her off, hoping there was some mistake. 'He's a bigger villain than Sligo! You know how he got his nickname "Toe-cutter", don't you? It's pretty self-explanatory.'

This was getting worse by the minute. Winter Frey was connecting me with another bad guy. I never thought I'd actually be talking to someone who knew both Vulkan Sligo and Toecutter Durham . . . although, ever since the run-in with that crazy guy back home, New Year's Eve, all I seemed to know was bad guys.

'Durham and Sligo were friends a really long time ago but now they're mortal enemies. I can't be caught having anything to do with anyone even remotely connected to Durham. Sligo would disown me. My life depends on it . . . well, my allowance depends on it.' Winter leaned forward and peered around the bushes towards the house. 'I probably need Sligo now just as much as he needs me.'

'Pocket money?' I asked.

She stifled a laugh. 'You could call it that. Anyway,' she added, 'it's easier doing it this way. To cut a long story short, my locket ended up with the bodyguard's girlfriend. I've been inside plenty of times before, and I know exactly where it is.'

The word 'locket' sent the hairs on the back of my neck prickling up. Sligo had asked me about a piece of jewellery—and someone had stolen jewellery from Dad's suitcase. Was this just a coincidence? Had this girl somehow got hold of it?

'And the locket's yours?' I asked her.

'That's what I just said. My mum and dad left it for me, for my tenth birthday.'

'So you didn't get it recently?'

'Yeah,' she said, rolling her eyes, 'I turned

ten yesterday! I just told you! What is this, an interrogation, or are you just a really bad listener? Anyway, the problem we have right now is the bodyguard . . . He's probably out working . . . but I'm not sure of that.'

'So we're breaking into Toecutter's bodyguard's house and he could be in there waiting for us?'

Winter nodded. 'Who's a clever boy?' she said in her mocking way. 'That's *exactly* it. Enough chitchat, let's get this thing over with.'

2:08 am

We were slowly approaching the huge double front doors, creeping up behind the bushes that lined the long driveway, when Winter tugged my arm, pulling me back. 'Not that way,' she hissed. 'Follow me.'

She led me around the side of the house, past huge curtained windows, until we came to a short flight of steps leading to a smaller door. She pulled out a credit card, slipped it between the door and the lock, gave it a deft tweak, and silently pressed it open.

I was impressed. Maybe I could learn a thing or two from her.

We crept into the house and stole down the

hall. I could hear the sound of a TV and I tapped Winter's shoulder. She turned to me, finger on her lips, and gestured ahead.

In the lounge room that opened up at the end of the hallway, a man—the bodyguard, I guessed—was sprawled on a black leather recliner with his back to us, in front of a huge plasma screen. On the thick, white rug at his feet slept the girl, curled up like a cat.

Winter pointed to the door on the other side of the room. We were going to have to sneak behind them and cross the room to get over there.

The guy was watching some war movie with lots of loud explosions, gunfire and shouting. I wondered how the hell the girl was sleeping through it. He seemed engrossed in the action but I didn't want to think about what he might do if he turned around and found two young intruders in his house.

Using the volume of the TV as cover, Winter and I pressed close against the wall and snuck through the lounge room, step by stealthy step. We slid our way along, silently passing only a metre or so behind the guy watching the movie. We had almost made it to the other side of the room when he suddenly turned—luckily not our way. Instead he glanced down the empty

hallway we'd just crept through. Had he heard
something?

Terrified that he would look round and see
us, we froze, but a child's scream from the movie
ripped his attention back to the screen.

After passing the last part of the wall we
slipped through the door and up some stairs. I
trailed Winter along a dimly lit, carpeted corridor, passing several closed doors and some huge
urns with spiky plants growing out of them.
Winter seemed to know exactly where to go.

After ducking into one of the rooms, Winter
quickly closed the door behind us and then
switched on a lamp. The light revealed a very
girly bedroom. The walls and curtains were a
soft pink, and the lace-white bed was covered in
cushions in every shade of pink you could imagine. Gabbi would have loved it.

Winter went straight for the dressing-table,
which was topped with a delicate glass-framed
mirror. She opened the top drawer and pulled
out a red velvet music box. Within seconds,
she'd silently lifted out a small, silver, heart-
shaped locket on a long chain. With a look of
triumph, she pocketed it, nodded to me, switched
off the lamp, and carefully opened the door
again.

We hurried out of the room and back down the staircase, treading softly on the carpet. We didn't need to go back through the lounge, so I hoped getting out of the house was going to be easier than getting in.

2:20 am

Winter opened the front door, but it slipped from her grasp and a gust of wind banged it against the wall behind.

'Who's there?!'

'What is it, hon?' came the girl's voice, dazed and sleepy on the rug.

'Someone's in the house!'

I didn't hesitate. This time *I* grabbed Winter and dragged her out of the front door, down the path and out through number 113's gate as fast as I could, only letting go of her wrist when we'd reached the street.

Her footsteps flew beside me as we raced along the road, taking left turns, then right, then left, until finally, when it was safe, we fell exhausted onto the grass of a tiny moonlit park.

We both puffed and panted, looking up at the sky.

'That damn front door!' she said, sitting up. 'I forgot it slams!'

She buried her hands into her skirt pockets

and pulled out two chocolate bars. She waved one around in front of me. I sat up and snatched it from her and started tearing off the wrapper.

'Thanks! Where'd you get these?'

'Let's just say I know where my *friend* keeps her chocolate stash, too,' she replied with a grin.

'It was pretty clear you'd been in there before.'

'I grew up in that house,' she said.

I remembered how she'd described her rich family before. 'Really?' I said. 'I've got an uncle who lives in this suburb, too.'

2:41 am

Winter's mobile rang, and she jumped up and took it out of her bag. I watched her move away to take the call and wondered who was ringing her at this hour.

'I'm getting a drink,' I said as Winter returned. I stood up on my aching legs and stumbled over to a water fountain in the middle of the park. I had a long drink and splashed water over my face and neck, trying to cool down. As I straightened up I found myself wondering how I could find out whether her story about the locket was true. Her sad eyes seemed so real, but there was something untrustworthy about her. I took another drink before heading back to where she sat on the grass, determined to find out more. In the light of the tall park lamp, I found Winter sitting there sifting through my backpack!

'Hey! Stop it!' I shouted, hurrying towards her. 'What are you doing? You can't do that! Get your hands off my stuff!'

Everything was scattered all over the grass, including Dad's drawings and the transparency I found in his suitcase with the words 'G'managh' and 'Kilfane'. I furiously started snatching my stuff up from the ground, when I noticed that she was sitting there quietly grinning. She held one of the angel drawings in her hands.

'Give me that!' I tried to grab it out of her hand, but she jerked it out of my reach.

I was about to give her a piece of my mind when I noticed her eyes. For the first time, they seemed alive and shining. She pointed to the angel, and pointed to my dad's letter.

'Where did this come from?' she asked. 'Do you know him too?'

'The angel?' I asked. 'You know about the angel?' A sudden surge of excitement smothered my anger.

'Of course I do! I know where he is. I've seen him lots of times!'

What was she talking about? Everybody in the whole freaking world seemed to be asking

questions about the angel and this girl was claiming she knew all about him!

'How long have you known about him?' she asked.

'I don't know about him, I've just got this picture that my dad drew. Why? What do you know? What does it mean?'

I didn't like the way Winter was handling Dad's drawing as if she owned it, so I snatched it away from her.

Winter's face resumed its usual cool, superior, stuff-you expression.

'Please,' I urged. 'Tell me everything you know about it.'

'Why? What's it to you?'

I sat back down on the grass again. 'My dad drew that angel not long before he died.'

The atmosphere immediately changed between us.

'Your dad's dead?' she asked.

I nodded.

Winter carefully pulled the locket out of her pocket. 'Now you understand,' she said in a softer voice, 'why this is so important to me.'

I did. I understood the way she clutched the locket, like it was the final word from a lost friend. It was the way *I* held Dad's drawings.

'You lost your dad, too, didn't you?' I asked.

Tears began to fill her eyes. She looked away without speaking . . . but I had my answer.

I wasn't lying when I said I knew how she felt. What kind of accident took the lives of both her mother *and* her father? I also knew that now wasn't the time to try and find out.

She remained silently turned away from me for a few moments, then she took the locket, opened it, and passed it to me. Inside were two tiny photos. One of an Asian man with black hair—whose intense eyes tilted up in the same way as Winter's—and opposite that, a photo of a fair-haired woman who had the same delicate chin as Winter.

'You look a lot like both of your parents,' I said, turning the locket over.

'Really?' she asked. 'It's hard to look like one or the other when your mum's so fair and your dad's Chinese.'

On the back of the silver heart were the delicately engraved words 'Little Bird' beneath a Chinese character.

At that moment, her mobile rang again. She took the locket back, then walked away to take the call.

I waited, wondering about her excitement at

Little Bird

seeing the angel drawing, wondering what had happened to her parents. Did she have a connection to the Ormond Angel? Winter owed me a lot of answers but I knew I'd have to be very careful and patient.

I couldn't hear what she was saying but it wasn't long before she was off the phone and back to me.

She looked me straight in the eyes. 'I've gotta go,' she said. 'He's hassling me again.'

'Sligo?'

'Thank God for mobiles,' she said. 'He thinks I'm at home. Clearly he's in a rage because you've disappeared, but he doesn't suspect I've had anything to do with it. Thank goodness. He likes to think he can keep tabs on me. As if. If only he knew where I really was, and who I was really with!'

'Listen,' I said quickly, not wanting the opportunity to slip by. 'I've got to find out about this angel. It's really important.' Even though I wasn't sure about this girl, I could feel the excitement growing in me at the thought of such an awesome break—I could be on the verge of finding out one of the secrets hidden in Dad's drawings.

'First, you've gotta tell me why it's so important to you,' she said. 'You tell me that, and I'll show you the angel *I* know.'

This girl hung out with criminals and broke into other people's houses. Was she telling the truth?

Winter was already walking away before I realised she was leaving.

'Hey! Come back!' I yelled after her.

'Only if you tell me why that angel is so important,' she called out. 'Why Sligo is willing to kill to get information about it.'

I didn't know what to say. If I told her about the Ormond Singularity and its connection to my dad's drawings, she could go straight to Sligo and tell him everything. I really wanted to trust her, but what I did know about her was telling me not to.

I jumped up and raced after her, catching her just before she'd reached the street a short distance away.

'You've gotta tell me where I can find that angel!'

She turned around and tossed her hair away from her face. 'I don't *gotta* do anything. No-one tells *me* what to do. You call me,' she said, 'when you're ready to deal. Then I'll consider it.'

She turned and hurried away.

'I don't even have your number!'

'Check your mobile, Callum Ormond!'

I ran to my backpack and pulled out my phone. It slid open to a new screensaver. Winter by moonlight, complete with a new phone number in my contacts list.

Hideout
38 St Johns Street

6:05 am

The birds were just beginning to call from the trees in the street as I crawled under the house and climbed up through the hole in the floorboards. The place smelled pretty foul and stuffy, so I opened the back door to get some fresh air inside.

I hadn't realised how starving I was until I

started eating. I ended up ploughing through half a loaf of stale bread.

I couldn't stop thinking about whether I could trust Winter. I desperately needed to find the angel that she said she knew about, but I couldn't bring myself to confide in her. I already had enough problems with Sligo and the woman who'd first abducted and interrogated me, who, for some reason, was stuck in my mind as a red-head. I couldn't risk them finding out anything more.

The little Celtic ring Gabbi had given me glinted on my finger. 'Get well, little Gabster,' I whispered, imagining her lying asleep in her intensive care bed.

I pulled out my sleeping-bag and crashed.

2:01 pm

'Dude, you're alive,' Boges said after I answered my phone.

'Only just.'

'I was trying to call you last night, but you must have been out of range. What happened, where were you?'

'Oh, long story . . .' I sighed, sitting up and stretching. The car yard was already a long-ago hazy blur.

'Nothing would shock me any more. You could tell me anything and I'd believe it.'

I could hear Mrs Michalko calling him in the background.

'Crap, I've gotta get off, Mum's coming,' he said. 'I'll drop by as soon as I can, OK.'

2 FEBRUARY

333 days to go . . .

5:17 pm

I'd spent the day holed up in the dump, trying again to make sense of the drawings and hoping for Boges to show up. I heard a couple of people talking and laughing as they walked by outside on the street, while I lurked in the dark, shifting about like a cockroach.

My plans to visit my great-uncle in Mount Helicon had completely fallen apart, thanks to Sligo, and while I really wanted to get out there and hopefully find some answers, I thought I was probably better off staying put for a few days.

Winter's mobile always seemed to be switched off, which was driving me nuts. What was the point of giving me her number if she was never going to take a call from me? I was sick and tired of having so many unanswered questions.

Feeling isolated and alone, I wished I could go home. I rang Mum once and left a message on her voicemail just so I could hear her voice and she could hear mine. I told her I was safe and not to worry.

I thought again of my little sister stuck in a hospital bed while Security watched out for her fifteen-year-old brother . . . They needed to be protecting her from people like the psycho woman and Sligo, who were all determined to discover Dad's secret and were willing to take out anyone in their path.

It wasn't fair: I'd done nothing wrong, but I was serving a sentence of solitary confinement, away from the people I needed to watch over. I just needed to stay alive long enough to solve Dad's mystery.

3 FEBRUARY

332 days to go . . .

2:11 am

I kept waking up, thinking I could hear Dad's
voice calling me.

I tossed and turned, not quite awake, but not
quite asleep either. Caught in that half-asleep
state I could see the threadbare toy dog from my
nightmares. It hovered in my mind, heavy and
bleak. I'd had so many close calls lately that I
couldn't understand why or how this image
could make me feel so uneasy. Storms at sea,
sharks, being thrown in a car boot, almost
drowning in oil—they were all terrifying things
I *could* understand.

9:33 am

My eyes flew open. Something had completely
wrenched me from sleep. I strained my ears to
hear a dull thudding that seemed to be coming

from outside. Straight away I thought of Winter, handing me and my secrets over to Sligo.

I crouched behind one of the boarded-up windows. Someone was definitely creeping around outside; I could hear their careful footsteps crushing the long grass.

I spotted the hole in the floor and dived into it, quickly pulling the carpet back over my head. Buried in dirt and cobwebs, I strained to hear where the footsteps had gone.

They'd stopped. Hunched under the floorboards I began crawling on all fours straight ahead towards the light and up behind the vegetation that grew around the front verandah.

I had to keep my head down low to avoid colliding with the sagging floor above. I cringed as my already-aching right shoulder slammed into a pylon.

The light ahead suddenly shifted, disappearing behind a figure crawling towards me! Someone was under the house with me!

Awkwardly, I started backing up. If I could make it back through the hole in the floorboards and drag something heavy over the opening, I'd be able to make a run for it. Unless there was someone waiting up there for me too.

'Dude? It's me!'

Boges!

'Cal?' he asked.

I peered ahead through the gloom under the house. As the dust settled I got a shock to find Boges's round face peering right back at me, centimetres from my own!

'Boges! Who else would be hiding down here in the dark?!'

9:37 am

'You almost gave me heart failure!' I continued.

'Sorry, dude. There was a police van cruising the street and I thought this way would be safer. Nice place you've got here,' he joked, wiping a sticky cobweb from his face.

Boges laughed at himself as we both pulled ourselves up into the house.

'Something smells damn good, for a change!' I said, as he opened his bag and threw me a squashed paper bag of sandwiches and chips. 'And they're still hot!'

'Yes, but don't forget to eat your fruit, young man,' he said in his best Mrs Michalko voice, tossing me a couple of apples and a banana.

'Oh, thanks, Mama M!' I joked.

He pulled his laptop out last, and then we made ourselves comfortable on the floor and got stuck into the food.

'What's the latest on Gabbi?' I asked.

Boges stopped chewing. 'No change. She's still unconscious. "Serious but stable."'

Stable. That word made everything sound a little bit better.

'And Mum?'

Boges made an indecisive groaning sort of sound. 'She's *kinda* OK. I went round to see her last night. She was complaining about one of your dad's colleagues—Eric somebody—saying how disappointed she was that he hadn't been in touch with her.'

'That'd be Eric Blair. He went to Ireland with Dad, but was working on another project.'

'He might be helpful to us,' suggested Boges. 'What's he like?'

'I spoke to him a couple of times on the phone, before passing him on to Dad, but that's all. He sounds like a nice guy. Dad seemed to like him. But you're absolutely right, he might be able to tell us more about what happened over there.'

'Definitely. So this Eric guy's in your mum's bad books, and as for you, well . . . she's still convinced you've had some sort of breakdown— that you're reacting to all the bad things that have happened to you. She even muttered something about knowing this day would come, and then when I asked her to explain what she meant, she acted like she hadn't said anything. It's weird, dude. I don't know, she just seems so . . . so vacant. It's like she's fighting something in herself, something that's telling her you're innocent. I told her you would never have done anything like that, I told her you *were* innocent, "Come on, Mrs O, it's Cal", and she just sort of patted my arm like she felt sorry for *me*.'

Boges looked at me with a helpless face. He started scratching his head. It was like he knew I needed to know what was going on, but he didn't want to be the one to tell me.

'Cal, I tried to tell her that your fingerprints were only on the gun because you picked it up when we were at your uncle's place, but it was useless. I could see she didn't want to listen to me. It's like she figures I'm making up stories to protect you, like I'm being stupid believing that my best friend is being wrongly accused. See, Rafe has said a few things about your "unstable mental state" and "recent aggressive behaviour" . . . and he's convinced you attacked Gabbi and that you were the one that shot him. How can you argue with that?'

'What's wrong with him? Unstable? Aggressive? He'd better not be talking about that day in the kitchen! I was just trying to grab *my* mail from him when the stupid idiot fell over himself. I didn't lay a finger on him. He lied about pinching the drawings then, and he's lying about this too.'

'But why would he lie about it?' said Boges, more like a statement than a question.

'I don't know. I think he's a loser and a liar, but I'd never hurt the guy.'

Boges picked up a handful of chips. 'Well, somebody did.'

'And whoever did that to Rafe also put my sister in a coma.' I swore and kicked at the leg of a broken chair. 'As if I would hurt them!'

'I know, I know, my friend. Chill out. But for whatever reason, that's what he thinks.'

'It just doesn't make sense.' I put my half-eaten sandwich down. 'He's lying. And no-one will believe me. Except you. Adults listen to adults. A kid's say means nothing.'

'Dude, it's not just a matter of his word. There's the matter of your fingerprints on the weapon.'

'Yeah, and like you already said, we both know how they got there. I just don't get it. We know it had to be his gun if it had my finger-prints on it. Maybe he knew something bad was coming. He could have been carrying it with him for protection—Oh, what's the point,' I said, frustrated with all the guessing.

We both sat back, staring at the ceiling.

'So . . . I'm afraid to ask . . .' said Boges hesitantly. 'What happened to you the other night—you said it was a "long story"?'

I'd kind of been hoping he wouldn't ask me that question. I sighed and gave him the rundown, starting with the casino explosion after we'd run away from Security at the Liberty Mall carpark, and then through to being tossed like useless trash into the underground oil tank.

11:02 am

'Trapped you in an oil tank!' shouted Boges. 'He was trying to drown you?!'

'Hey, keep it down! Yes, an oil tank. I thought I was dead. The oil had fully covered my mouth and just when I was thinking this is it, someone turned off the pump and the tank stopped filling.'

'Who? Who stopped it?'

'A girl.'

'A girl?! What?'

'Her name's Winter Frey. She says Vulkan Sligo's her guardian . . .' I could see Boges growing suspicious, fast. 'Apparently he used to work for her dad, I don't know how long ago. Her parents were pretty cashed-up but they both died in some sort of accident, and she's been in the care of the Slug ever since.'

'So if she's with him, why did she save you?' Boges wanted to know.

'I don't know.' I wanted to know the answer to that question too. 'Maybe she just couldn't sit back knowing I was about to die.' She must have been watching it happen from a hiding place.

'I think she relies on him to get by,' I continued, 'but I don't think she's into his gangster lifestyle—you know, drowning teenagers and stuff. She reckons he's on a serious mission to become acceptable—some sort of pillar of society.'

Boges looked like he was about to choke after my 'pillar of society' comment.

'I know,' I continued. 'What kind of pillar of society kills people . . . but Winter says Sligo believes the Ormond Singularity will make him famous. If he can work it out. I turned out to be a less-than-helpful source of information for him, but at least I know now that I've got two criminal gangs chasing this thing. Winter says she's willing to help me but I think she may be doing it to collect favours. Get people in debt to her so that she can call on them when she needs something.'

Boges sat back quietly and listened as I explained the break-in to get Winter's locket, and the claims she made in the park about recognising my dad's angel drawings.

'Do you believe her? That she knows where the angel is?' he asked.

I remembered her shining face; that sort of thing can't be faked.

'I'm convinced of it. She really came alive when she saw the drawings,' I said. 'She promised she'd take me to see it.'

Boges had made himself comfortable on the floor near the wall, his round face serious again. 'But she's got an agenda of her own, wanting to know why the angel is important to you.'

'She saved my life, Boges. So I'm willing to take some risk on her—even though she's one weird girl. She's nothing like any of the girls we know, but I kind of like that about her. And, anyway, as we've said before, the angel is important. Dad drew him twice, so I think she's our best chance at the moment.'

'She hot?'

'What?'

'Winter. She's hot, isn't she?'

'She's OK,' I said, awkwardly. Normally I'd be pretty open with Boges about girls, but something made me want to keep that part of Winter to myself.

Boges gave me a look. 'Right. If she starts working things out we could be in real trouble. Be on your guard, dude. We don't want another rival, or enemy, after the same thing. Especially not someone connected to that lunatic Sligo. You've already got two very dangerous enemies.'

At least, I thought to myself.

'Try her number again,' said Boges.

The mobile you have dialled is switched off. Please try again later.

Boges opened his laptop. 'No-one knows about this either. Someone chucked it out because it had stopped working, but it only needed a new power box,' he said. 'The motherboard was fine. But, before we start busting our brains on those drawings again, let's get your profile underway.'

'I already have a profile,' I said gloomily. 'At every cop shop.'

'I think you should start a blog,' he said. 'An appeal to the public could be helpful.'

'A blog? Like MySpace?'

'Yeah. A place where you can try and get across your side of the story, and shut down all the crazy stuff the media's saying about you. Nobody has to see you or know where you are. They can just read what you have to say and judge for themselves.'

'Great idea. Boges, you're a genius.'

'I know.'

'And modest, too.'

For a second it was like the old days, when I was just another kid mucking round with a mate. That feeling didn't last long, but at least I had a little hope, and a chance to tell the world of my innocence.

1:04 pm

In the time it took to set up my profile, I'd forgotten about tricky Winter, until I looked over at my phone and saw her face looking up at me. I stretched my leg out and carefully kicked it under my bag.

'I can't stay much longer,' Boges reminded me, glancing at his watch. 'I've already skipped all my morning classes. Don't want to start bringing in too many notes *from Mum* this term.'

Boges could forge his mother's signature perfectly.

I never thought I would envy someone going to school, but I would have done anything to be packing my bag and heading off with Boges. I'd happily have sat through the 'Welcome back' assembly in the hall—all the 'over-the-holiday updates' and 'hopes for the year ahead' speeches—that would normally have bored me to tears. I'd even have happily sat through one of Mr Lloyd's biology classes, listening to him drawl on and on about lab safety in his boring, monotone voice, while I helped Boges conduct his own little groundbreaking experiments up the back. Or Mrs Hartley's English class, and her long-winded soliloquies on Shakespeare and poetry.

'I don't think anyone wants to hear my side of the story,' I said. 'The cops have made up their minds about me already and we both know that Mum and Rafe think I'm some sort of dangerous nutcase.'

'They're worried about you, that's for sure,' said Boges.

'And I'm worried about Mum. I can't help but wish Rafe would keep away from her.'

'I guess she relies on him now that your dad's gone,' said Boges. 'And he *is* your dad's brother.'

'Just because he looks exactly the same as Dad,' I said, 'doesn't mean anything. Whenever he's around, bad things happen. He pinched the drawings and lied about them. Now he's got me in this mess, Boges. Why does he want me out of the way?'

'Come on, we've got no proof of that. I don't think it's Rafe that's got you into this mess; I just think he hasn't really helped get you out of it. But think about it, he's had a rough time too. He lost his twin brother. He almost drowned in Treachery Bay. You know, he could have been *killed* at your place that day. And he's got a heart condition, hasn't he? His niece is in a coma. His nephew's on the run from the law. His sister-in-law is on the verge of a nervous break-down, and he's the only one around trying to keep it all together. Nobody else has stepped up. This can't be easy for him either, Cal. I've seen him at your mum's place, and he looks like a wreck.'

'You may be right. He's so damn cold all the time, I forget that he may just have a heart in there.'

'I don't blame you. Anyway,' said Boges, picking up his mobile and steering me towards the bathroom where the light was a little brighter, 'let's take a quick profile shot. This dump won't give your whereabouts away, but you'd better turn your face a little,' said Boges, 'so that most of you is in shadow.'

Like my life is now. In the shadows.

Boges pointed the phone at me and took a photo.

'That'll do. I'll upload it all now.'

'I hope Mum sees this,' I said.

'I'll make sure she does,' said Boges.

'Maybe she'll change her mind about me.'

Boges nodded, but I could tell he was just being nice.

'The cops will see it, eventually,' he said, 'but it won't help them. We'll just need to be really careful about where and when we post messages.'

Boges started to pack up his gear. 'I'll come round again on the weekend,' he said. 'Oh, and I almost forgot, I bought this for you to keep the drawings in.'

He handed me a strong, rigid plastic folder, with a clip seal down one side. 'Keep them in this. They're going to fall apart unless they're properly protected.'

He paused and I could see he had something on his mind.

'What?' I asked, taking the folder from him.

'Man,' he said, picking up his laptop, 'be careful, OK? I mean it. Don't think you're safe even for a second because you're not. I hate to say

Web | Images | Video | News | Maps | More ∨

[   ] **Web Search**

Hello, Callum

Contact Cal
Messages for Cal

Male
15 years old
Richmond

My name is Cal Ormond. I'm 15 and I *used* to go to Richmond High. I'm sure you've heard about me from TV and the papers. Forget it all; nothing they're saying about me is true. I am innocent.

I love my little sister Gabbi and would never do anything to hurt her. I did not attack my uncle, Rafe. I have no reason to hurt him. I walked into my house last month and found both of them unconscious. I ran to Gabbi and gave her CPR until she was breathing again. I never thought I'd ever have to do CPR for real. I was being chased, so I had to run as soon as the ambulance and police turned up.

Can you imagine finding your little brother or sister unconscious on the floor? It was the worst thing I've ever seen, and lately I've seen a lot. Now she's in a coma and I can't even visit her and tell her it's going to be OK.

Ever since my dad died last year, heaps of bad things have happened to me. My uncle and I nearly drowned in Treachery Bay, because our fishing boat had been sabotaged. Our house was trashed, and then there were the violent attacks on Gabbi and Rafe. My family is being targeted and I don't know why. It's not just the cops that are after me, but it's not safe for me, or my family, if I say any more than that.

Inbox
Update Profile
Sign Out

I'm on the run and everyone thinks I'm the bad guy. I am *not* a dangerous person and I did not hurt my uncle or my sister. Please believe me. I need people on my side. All I want to do is clear my name and stay alive so that I can look after my family. That's all I want. Please, if you know anything at all that might help my case, contact me here before it's too late.

POSTED BY TEENFUGITIVE AT 1:31 PM   0 Messages it, but I don't want to add you to the list of tragedies.'

'I know. I'm no good to anyone if I'm dead.'

'I'm willing to do anything to help. You know that. I think this blog is a good move, but just remember that it's never too late to come in from the cold. I don't want to lose the best buddy a guy ever had. You want to run with it, I'm with you. You want to drop the whole thing, I'm with you, too. So ask yourself . . . are you totally sure you want to persist with this? Unravelling your dad's secret? Now that you're starting to realise the full extent of the danger?'

In the dim light of the derelict house, Boges's words sounded ominous, almost frightening: *The full extent of the danger.* I'd made a promise to myself when I was back in my old house, looking into the eyes of my dad in the family photo, and I wasn't going back on it.

'There's no way I can turn back now,' I said. 'It's what keeps me going.'

'Keeps you going? I never picked you for a thrill-seeker,' said Boges, unsmiling.

'Far from it. I just know that I'd be no good to anyone in juvenile detention either.'

I looked around the dump I was living in. 'The only thing I've got going for me is the *truth.*

I know it's dangerous, but while ever there's the chance to solve the mystery of the Ormond Singularity and clear my name, I must do it. I *have* to do it. Otherwise I'm going to be on the run all my life.'

7 FEBRUARY

328 days to go . . .

4:03 pm

I'd given up trying to ring Winter, convinced that she had given me a dud number. I was beginning to think that she had just been stringing me along with her talk of knowing about the angel. Who knew whether any of the stories that this girl had spun really happened as she told them.

True to his word, Boges arrived, climbing up through the floor again. I'd been dying to see him, not only just to have some company, but to find out whether my blog had gone up live OK.

'It's up and running,' Boges assured me, 'and you're getting heaps of hits!'

I felt better hearing that. Not quite so cut off from the world. 'Has anyone posted anything yet?'

'Not yet, but I think it's just a matter of some-one making that first move—people are probably a bit nervous about it. But I reckon once you get that first comment, hundreds will follow. I'll let you know when it happens.'

Boges pulled out the little black leather notebook that he carried with him everywhere—it was filled with his middle-of-the-night ideas, complicated sketches and almost-indecipherable notes, and was held together by a string of elastic. 'I've been meaning to tell you about the info I found on the net about the Ormond Riddle.

'The Ormond Riddle Society is dedicated to the fostering and performance of Tudor and Renaissance music,' he read. 'It's not great—like that was from some singing group's website.'

He was right, that wasn't great news.

'Another website explained that the Ormond Riddle,' Boges continued, 'was thought to have been written by a famous Tudor musician, William Byrd. But there wasn't anything there on the actual words . . . or music . . . or what-ever it is we're looking for. I'll search again when I get a chance. In the meantime, can we take another look at the drawings?'

'Sure.' I lifted the drawings out from under some loose floorboards, emptied the folder and spread them onto the floor. Boges pointed to the image of the Sphinx, tapping his finger on the

pencil drawing of the crouching mythical beast and the Roman guy in front of it.

'I've been reading up on the Sphinx and Egypt,' he said, 'trying to work out why your dad might have drawn it. I don't know what *this* drawing means, exactly, but I did find out something interesting.'

'Yeah?' I prompted. 'Spit it out.'

'The Sphinx is connected with a riddle.'

'A *riddle*?' A charge of energy made me sit up straight. 'Now that *is* interesting. The riddle of the Sphinx and the Ormond Riddle.'

'Your dad had riddles on the brain and I bet he knew about the Ormond Riddle. Maybe he even knew the words. Is there anyone else in your family who might know something?'

'Maybe one of my old relatives can help—the

great-uncle or great-aunt. I didn't get out to Great-uncle Bartholomew's, as planned, but he's probably my best shot.'

I didn't have much family. Dad's parents had died long ago and Mum's few relatives lived overseas.

'Do you think Dad was trying to suggest that the secret he was onto—the Ormond Singularity—had something to do with solving the Ormond Riddle?'

'Yes, and that's why I've checked the dictionary for exactly what *riddle* means.'

'Isn't it kind of like a joke? Some sort of trick?'

'Listen and learn, dude,' said Boges, reading from his notebook yet again. 'According to the dictionary, a riddle is "a question or a statement requiring thought to answer or understand; something perplexing, something that requires solving; an enigma."'

'A what?'

'Yeah, I had to look that one up too. "An enigma is something secret or hidden,"' said Boges.

'We already knew that!' I said in frustration. 'Take a look at them; they're *all* enigmas!'

'Hang on a minute. You wouldn't have known anything about a riddle if you hadn't seen the words "Ormond Riddle" in your uncle's office. Your dad wasn't to know you'd get that bit of information,' he said, getting up and packing up his things.

'I just wish Dad'd told us something a bit more helpful.'

'Dude,' said Boges, his round face suddenly very serious, 'look what we're up against. Your dad knew he had to be very careful conveying this information to you, and that was before his mind went on him. You're lucky he managed the drawings.'

Boges flipped the elastic back around his note-book and slipped it into his pocket. 'Of course, he was also counting on me being here to help you figure it all out. I mean, seriously, what would you do without me?'

'I don't know whether it's your brain or your modesty that I like best, Boges.'

'I can imagine, dude. It must be tough keeping up with me. And don't think for a second I'm boasting about my talent. It's just a fact.'

He was only mucking around, but it was true. At school Boges came first, year after year, in just about every subject. And then of course there was all his electronic stuff, completely self-taught. He could take any old piece of junk off the street and have it functioning again in no time. He'd once built a robotic backpack on caterpillar treads that 'walked' along behind him to school and into the classroom. He'd made and sold quite a few, until the teachers banned them when they realised Boges had really just designed them so he could stage monster-truck-style crashes with the other kids in the corridors.

'Between us,' said Boges, 'we'll work it out. When I get home from school, I'm going to track down who this Roman is, and have another search for the Ormond Riddle on the net. I'm also going to see if "Ormond Angel" takes me anywhere.'

'Good idea.'

I looked at the strong features of the drawing of the Roman, the way the hair hung over the guy's forehead, the thick nose and empty eyes. It looked just like one of those marble heads that you'd see in a museum. I thought I understood the Sphinx. But together with the head? It made no sense.

Sirens started wailing out on the street. I jumped up and hurried over to peer through a crack near the door.

I jumped back in fear. 'Cops! There are cops out on the street!'

'Uh-oh, I hope they didn't follow me,' whispered Boges. 'I was so careful—always am.'

He squinted through the crack just as I had done. 'There's a police van across the road,' he said, turning round. 'If they see me coming out of here and someone recognises me . . .'

'Quick! Under the house,' I said, grabbing the drawings and shoving them back into the plastic folder.

Boges jumped first and then I crawled down after him. This time we carefully made our way to the back of the house and underneath the verandah.

Beyond a small clearing directly in front of the verandah, the garden had turned into a jungle where creepers had almost completely smothered the bushes and small trees. We forced our way through it to the old back fence.

'Gotta go,' said Boges. 'Mum'll be wondering where I am—I promised I'd take her shopping. You know what she's like with her English.'

'That's cool, but come back soon. You know I can't do this without you.'

'Aw, shucks,' joked Boges, his round face grinning wide like a Halloween pumpkin. He pressed a twenty-dollar note into my hand. 'And here's me thinking you didn't care!'

I gave him a quick jab, which he returned, then he climbed the fence and disappeared.

7:11 pm

I waited under the house, watching the cops across the road for about an hour. It seemed like there was some kind of domestic dispute over there, and nothing at all to do with me and my hideout.

Back inside, I tried to focus on all the information I had so far from the drawings. We had a collection of things that could be worn, a blackjack, something that seemed to point to the Ormond Riddle . . .

Then, of course, there was a certain someone who claimed to know more about the drawings of the angel.

I had to get more information from her. I had to take a chance.

9 FEBRUARY

326 days to go . . .

Car yard

9:04 am

With my hoodie pulled right down over my face, I risked making my way back to Sligo's car yard. I'd tossed and turned about it for a couple of nights, but had no choice; I didn't know where else to start looking for Winter, and I had to speak to her. Time was ticking.

I hid behind some bushes across the road from the main entrance and although I saw people coming and going, including the stocky guy with the red singlet who had tossed me in the tank, I didn't see any sign of her.

It was a much bigger establishment than I'd first realised. Most of it had been in darkness when Sligo had captured me. I'd only seen the office and laundry area and the closely-surrounding yard under light. Everything between there and running for the gate was a haze.

Deeper into the lot there were long lines of cars under tarpaulins and a number of small sheds filled with engine parts and engine blocks.

I was about to leave, after an hour or so of monitoring the place, when a sudden movement caught my eye. Over in the left-hand corner of the yard, near the road, someone was scampering up and over the fence. I sat up, alert. Someone was sneaking into Sligo's car yard! They must have been pinching spare parts! The thief was safe with me—there was no way I'd be running to the boss to tell him about it. I could see the figure more clearly as he quietly made his way further in; it was a kid wearing boots, jeans and a dark brown hoodie, and he seemed to be creeping along the rows of covered cars, looking for something in particular. As he lifted the tarpaulins, one by one, I could see that many of the cars had been in bad crashes, their bumper bars crushed, wheels and axles bent at odd angles. I guessed the kid was looking for a part from a specific make and model.

It was an unusual feeling being the quiet witness for once instead of the one trying to get on with business without being caught. The kid jumped down from a car not too far from me and when he stood up . . . I saw that he was actually a *she*!

Her slim figure quickly dropped to the ground again and off she went, crawling along the rows of cars, lifting tarpaulins, dropping them and then proceeding to the next wreck.

As I stood up to leave, she must have noticed the movement and swung around to see who was watching her. I was quicker and dropped back down behind my cover, peering once more through the bushes.

The girl frantically scanned the street and then, satisfied that no-one was there, she continued with her search.

Slowly I got to my feet and backed away, completely puzzled.

What on earth was Winter Frey doing creeping around Sligo's car yard?

12 FEBRUARY

323 days to go . . .

Hideout
38 St Johns Street

12:13 pm

Winter had been on my mind even more since I spotted her at the car yard. What was she doing there, sneaking around? Did she have a little side business of her own—stealing spare parts from Sligo and then selling them elsewhere? I'd wanted to call out to her—I'd gone there to find her—but I knew she would have just run away from me. And she would *not* have been happy about being sprung . . .

I looked at her number in my phone, frustrated that I could never reach her on it. I shoved it back into my bag.

It had been a few days since I'd last seen Boges and I hadn't been able to get a hold of him either.

'Boges!' I said, after practically diving across the room to answer my phone before it stopped ringing.

'I know, I'm sorry, I haven't been able to talk the last couple of days, but anyway, dude, I have some news.'

'Has something happened to Mum or Gabbi?' I asked, my chest pounding.

'Gabbi, I'm sorry to say, is much the same,' said Boges. 'Your mum's fine, but . . .'

'But what?'

'She's moving into Rafe's place.'

My heart sank. I knew it was probably going to happen sooner or later, with our house already up for rent, but I'd been hoping some sort of miracle would solve Mum's money problem before any decisions like that'd have to be made.

'I knew you wouldn't be happy about it,' said Boges, 'but, hey, I checked your blog and it looks good—you've got some messages now.'

'Really?'

'A few people are having their say about you. Yeah, you've got your regular dose of crazies in there, but some are definitely on your side. Well, two, at least. Real hotties: Tash and Jasmine.'

I felt a smile creep up on my face. Cute names, I thought.

'What did they say?'

'Just that they could tell you weren't a bad guy, and that everyone should be innocent until proven guilty,' he said.

I nodded to myself, feeling great that two girls I didn't even know believed in me.

'And then,' continued Boges, 'they said that they thought you were pretty hot and that they'd like to protect you from the real bad guys . . .'

'What?'

'I'm serious! That's what they said. It's amazing what a life of crime can do for a guy!'

Boges fumbled with the phone for a moment. 'If you were here you'd see that I've got my hand up and I'm waiting for a high-five. Come on, don't leave me hanging!'

We both cracked up laughing.

'I think it might even be helping *my* popularity,' said Boges. 'Madeleine Baker sat next to me in the art studio this morning.'

'No way!'

'First she said that she really liked my metal spider sculpture from last year, at least until I designed that program for it and it got away . . .'

'Yeah, right out the school gates and under a bus!'

'Then Maddy said that it must have been so

hard on me, finding out that my best friend was . . .' Boges hesitated.

'Was what?'

'. . . a psycho.' I could hear Boges shuffling about uncomfortably. 'Sorry, I didn't mean to bring that up. I told her that it didn't bother me a bit—you weren't a psycho, and that it would just be a matter of time before everyone else understood that.'

I hated hearing that, but it wasn't surprising. I knew very well what everyone was thinking about me. My own mother thought I was a monster.

'So she ended up sitting somewhere else?' I asked.

'No, she didn't actually. We're now paired up for a photography project. We'll be sitting together all term, whether we want to or not!'

'If you were here you'd see that my hand's up and ready for a high-five, Boges. Come on, don't leave me hanging!'

We both laughed again.

I wanted to see the blog comments for myself. Maybe even add some of my own. I decided I'd check it all out at an internet café as soon as it was safe.

'I think this whole blog thing is great, but it's also caused a lot of flak,' said Boges. 'The Police

Commissioner was on the news last night saying
that they wouldn't be shutting your page down.
They're hoping to trace you. To luck onto information that will lead them to you.'

'I'm not going to slip up and give anything
away. But can they trace me electronically?'

'It would be very hard to do. I've done a lot of
fancy footwork to make it near-impossible.'

'You're a legend, Boges. Thanks.'

I could hear the distant sound of hundreds of
kids fooling around in the schoolyard coming
down the phone line.

'I think I've given up on Winter,' I said. 'Her
phone's still switched off.'

'Might be just as well,' said Boges. 'She's
part of Sligo's mob. How do you know they're
not a team? You know, like playing good cop,
bad cop.'

'What are you saying?'

'I've been thinking about it. That whole thing
in the oil tank could have been a set-up. Sligo
pretends to try and kill you, then she pretends
to save you when all seems lost, so you tell her
all your secrets out of gratitude. But all the time
she's reporting back to the big guy.'

'Boges, I really don't think so. I was seconds
away from death when she stopped the oil pump.'

'Don't you see?' Boges asked. 'That's what

they want you to believe. You start to trust her and let your guard down and then you open up all about the drawings, your dad's letter, the empty jewel case . . . and they add all that to what they already know . . . It works heaps better than drowning you in sump oil.'

I thought about it for a moment. Boges could have been right. And I hadn't even told him about spotting her snooping around the car yard.

'But we don't know what they might know already,' I said.

'Exactly,' said Boges. 'And that's why you have to be extra cautious.'

There was a sudden sound out the front of the house. I dropped to the floor. 'Gotta go,' I whispered. 'There's someone outside the house.'

The sound came again—a ripping, tearing sound. Someone was wrenching the boards off the front door, trying to get inside!

I swore down the phone. 'Boges, I've gotta go!'

Not caring how much noise I made, I grabbed the folder with the drawings inside and stuffed everything into my backpack, then pushed it through the hole in the floorboards. The sound of splintering wood filled the air.

I took a quick glance around, and hoping I hadn't left any incriminating material lying about, I dived through the hole in the floor-boards, twisting back to pull the carpet off-cut back into position over the opening.

Panting, I crawled under the house, making my way through the dense growth to where Boges had made his escape before.

3:19 pm

I drove myself through the jungle of leaves and branches, launched over the back fence, swung myself over into the neighbour's yard, and hit the ground running.

There was yelling and shouting behind me but I just kept ducking and weaving, putting street after street between me and the St Johns house.

Deserted railway yard

3:52 pm

I stopped running in the west of the inner city, near the railway. Sweat poured down my body as I squeezed through a fence into a deserted area where old railway sheds and rusting carriages stood, separated by thick grass growing high between them. I practically collapsed on the ground, hidden under an old carriage, hoping that the intruders had not been the cops.

4:04 pm

It didn't look like the yards had been used in years. I scanned for security cameras. I couldn't see any—there wasn't really anything there that needed protecting from thieves—but I kept my head down, anyway.

4:43 pm

When the coast was clear I crawled out and began investigating the area more closely. Not far from my hiding place there was a deep drain: a cement canal that followed the sloping land. I jumped down into it and followed it until I came to the opening of a huge pipe culvert that must have directed the stormwater underground. It was like the opening of a railway tunnel, only a third of the size. It was barred, but the bars had been bent, allowing me to squeeze through them quite easily.

Further in, the cement floor of the tunnel sloped away into darkness. This might be a good place to lie low for a while, I thought. I dug around in my backpack and pulled out my torch. The light revealed graffiti-covered walls. Some of the tags I recognised from around the city. There were two that dominated all the others:

WHEN iT RAINS NO DRAINS

no psycho

It hadn't rained in ages so I didn't have to worry about the first warning. But the second one troubled me. It was one I'd seen a lot of in the last couple of weeks and I hoped there *was* 'no psycho' lurking down in the darkness with me. Me and the rats . . .

I walked on.

5:23 pm

I could no longer see the light behind me from where I'd entered the tunnel, and was surrounded in darkness. I flashed my torch around to see that the graffiti and the tagging had thinned out. Obviously not many people were keen to venture this far into the drain.

5:36 pm

I came to an intersection where the stormwater drain had widened and split into a Y-shape, now with two drains leading further into the dark. Just above head height, my torchlight revealed two deep recesses in the walls of the drain, one on each side, possibly for the maintenance workers to store stuff. I flashed the torch around to check out both of them, deciding that the one on the left looked drier. No-one could see me if I was up there and kept hard up against the wall. I could camp up there. I'd hear people coming— their footsteps would echo loudly down to me—and I'd be able to get out well before they reached me by disappearing down one of the smaller channels.

I threw my backpack up first and carefully placed the torch up there to give me light. I got a good grip with my fingers and hauled myself up there. The rockclimbing I'd done with Dad in the past helped.

I spread myself out on my sleeping-bag, ripped open a packet of biscuits, and started thinking about the people from my blog who, for whatever reason, believed in me.

And I thought of that strange girl, Winter, and wondered again what game she was playing. I hoped Boges was wrong about her.

9:00 pm

I woke up, sore and cramped.

I needed to do something. I couldn't just keep moving from hole to hole. I was almost halfway through month number two. I was warned I needed to survive 365 days—how far in was I? My brain was too messy even to work that simple subtraction out.

Bottom line was that this nightmare wasn't going to resolve itself. If Winter wasn't going to help me, the only place I could think of hunting down information was the house I'd escaped from after the first kidnapping.

I needed to know more about my enemies. I'd have to stop being the hunted and instead hunt *them* down.

10:20 pm

Hurrying along the dark roads I searched for familiar street names, buildings, houses, anything that I recognised from my long run home after escaping from the first kidnapping. I was determined to find the house where I'd been held again and although I'd only seen a small part of the front entrance, the tiles and the inside of the broom cupboard, I felt confident that if I saw it again, I'd know it.

But finding the right street—that was another matter altogether.

10:52 pm

A couple of times I thought I'd seen something familiar but wasn't led anywhere. I was looking for a particular intersection that I remembered seeing not long after escaping from the broom cupboard. It had a small church on one corner, a twenty-four-hour carwash with a couple of pinball machines in it on another, and on the other side was the large fenced-off area of a school playground.

I felt like I was getting warmer.

11:23 pm

I was thinking about having to face the long walk back to the drains if I hadn't made any progress, when I squinted, straining to see if the little building I was approaching was in fact the church I was looking for.

On the right was a carwash and a schoolyard, dark, empty and eerily lit by the street lights. I hurried closer.

I'd found the intersection!

I stood on the edge of the kerb at the front of the church and tried to take myself back to that night—I'd been so filled with fear and adrenaline at the time it was a wonder I remembered anything.

I recalled the distinct sandstone kerbing that I'd stumbled on as they'd dragged me, sack slipping from my head, out of the car, and so I began running down the road alongside the church, searching the driveways to find a match. I quickly passed the houses, giving each one a good look, until finally, through the front gates of a large place, I recognised the paving I'd stumbled on. I jumped back as a car made its way down the street and continued past me.

Quietly I climbed over the fence, slipped up the driveway and took cover behind some big recycling bins. There was a four-wheel drive parked under a carport. The inside of the house was completely dark. There weren't any lights on. Hopefully that meant no-one was up.

I looked around for any other signs that this was the place I was after, but only found some little kids' bikes leaning up against the carport wall. I crept up and peered into the car. A bruised apple, sunscreen, some baby wipes and a booster seat.

I had to be in the wrong place . . .

13 FEBRUARY

322 days to go . . .

12:08 am

It was now after midnight. I had trusted my instincts and decided to move on. Back out on the street I restarted my search for the sandstone kerbing.

Sure enough, a hundred metres or so up the road, I found another sandstone driveway and big, open front gate. I crept up and squatted beside a plumbing van that was parked next door, so I could try and get a better look.

There were soft voices and signs of movement. I strained to pinpoint where they were coming from.

A car door closing. *It was the dark blue Mercedes from the kidnapping!*

Someone fumbling with keys.

A woman's heels clicking on the paving stones, followed by dull, heavier footsteps.

Two people—one of them a woman wearing a spotty scarf around her head, and a large man's figure in shadow—were making their way from the car to the front door.

From my vantage point I watched as they went inside, lights switching on to indicate where in the house they'd moved to.

The house was heavily secured with metal bars over the lower windows and a thick security door at the front. I was feeling pretty sure I'd found the right place, but how was I ever going to get inside?

12:19 am

Beside the house was a very tall pine tree that had recently been lopped; its lower limbs had been cut back from the driveway near the entrance and almost formed a natural 'ladder' that was just asking me to climb it.

12:22 am

The branches scratched my face and hands on the climb up and the mosquitoes were hammering me, too, but I could now see clearly into the house through an open window near the verandah on the first floor.

And there inside were the red and black tiles that I'd stood on while I was interrogated by that deranged woman!

The door inside the main room in my view

opened and in came two people. The woman had removed her scarf and her crimson-red hair was piled up high in an elaborate hairstyle. Crimson-red! How had I known this without ever seeing her before? I'd barely seen anything but the floor during the abduction and interrogation, and yet for some reason I'd remembered her as a woman with red hair . . . the exact woman behind the desk that I was staring at through the pine needles!

She leaned into a drawer, and then pulled out a long, thin brownish cigarette—a cigarillo. Smoke filled the room and began floating up and out of the window towards me. I held my breath.

She was talking to the man who had accompanied her from the car, who was now standing on the other side of the desk. His suit jacket strained against his bulging body. He looked like a big exercise ball wearing clothes. The red-head's unforgettable voice was loud and distinct, strong and aggressive. She was gesturing with her hands and stabbing the air with the cigarillo as if she were making important points. He too seemed to have a lot to say and they were both very interested in some papers on the desk in front of her.

From the way she dominated the room and conversation, I knew this was the woman who had questioned me the night I was abducted from

Memorial Park. I remembered the way Sligo had reacted when I'd described her to him, the way he'd spat and then ground his heel on the wet spot. He knew very well who she was.

I pulled out my phone, wishing the camera function had better zoom. Luckily the room was fairly well lit, so I didn't need my flash. I quickly took the best picture I could of the woman. It wasn't great, but I'd definitely captured her basic shape and features. She was a unique character so I was hoping that someone, somewhere, might recognise her.

Inside, the woman crushed out the cigarillo and opened a tall glass jar on her desk filled with tiny silver balls. She popped a few in her mouth and I recognised them as being the cachous that Gabbi loved using to decorate cupcakes. She then opened a laptop in front of her. The computer screen radiated bluish light onto her face. I wondered again whether she was the woman who'd first called me claiming to have information on my dad . . . and then set me up. Was she *Jennifer Smith*?

From behind the laptop she suddenly called the big guy over with a dramatic flap of her arms. He rushed to her side and leaned in to see whatever it was on the screen that was so intriguing. They stared at each other for a moment, quite intently, and before I knew it the red-head had turned and was peering out of the window right at me!

12:35 am

I instantly dropped heavily to the ground and my movement must have activated an automatic spotlight—the garden was lit up like a football stadium at night. I ran down the driveway and into the darkness. I didn't pause to listen to what was going on behind me; all my energy was focused on getting the hell out of there.

I ran back down the street towards the intersection and then back the way I'd come.

When I'd run far enough and figured it was safe, I stopped to see if anyone was on my trail.

Nothing.

I strained to listen for a car, voices, footsteps . . .

Nothing.

No-one was chasing me. I was running without a pursuer. Had they seen me? I was sure the woman had looked right at me! Did they have security cameras outside? Was I completely paranoid? Had I fled for no reason?

Whatever the case, I'd found the house, taken a picture of the woman, and made it out of there in one piece.

14 FEBRUARY

321 days to go . . .

Stormwater drain

10:10 am

I'd spent a whole day lurking in the drain. Boges wasn't going to manage meeting up with me for another day or two, so I'd tried to keep busy walking up and down the tunnels, rifling through my stuff, sleeping, staring at the ceiling . . . talking to myself.

I had to get out again.

Central Station

11:29 am

Now I was just another anonymous kid wandering the streets near Central Station. Nothing unusual about that. Or so I kept telling myself.

I tried to act calm and cool, and remain unnoticed, but I felt like a hundred pairs of eyes were on me.

I stopped by a basketball court where a bunch of kids were having a shootout. I'd always liked playing basketball—or any sport, really—and wished I had it in me to go over and play with them.

All of a sudden I felt the hairs at the back of my neck prickling up. Someone *was* watching me. I was sure of it. I swung round, but there was no-one there. I turned my attention back to the basketball court and that's when I got the shock of my life!

There was a kid on the other side of the netted-off court staring at me through the mesh! But that wasn't what had frozen me.

I stared back in disbelief!

Was I seeing things?

He looked as shocked as I did, which didn't help.

My brain tried to make sense of it. Was I looking at some sort of reflection? I rubbed my eyes like a spun-out cartoon character, but when I looked again, he was still there.

He was the spitting image of me—or, at least, what used to be me. My face, my body, my eyes, my nose, my jaw, my eyebrows. *My* face!

My face before I had to try and make myself look unrecognisable.

I stared again. He still looked just like me, and he was still staring right back at me.

I was spellbound.

I finally snapped myself out of it and shouted to him.

'Hey!' I yelled, as I started to run around the sides of the court, trying to get to him. The moment I started running, so did he. But he was running *away* from me.

He took off, legs and arms pumping, like he was running for his life. It was like some bizarre out-of-body experience, like seeing *me* running for *my* life a month ago.

'Hey! Wait!' I called after him.

But he wouldn't look back. He just kept running. I kept on after him, watching him try to duck and weave and lose me in the crowds, through narrow alleys and laneways. They were all the tricks I'd come to know so well.

I was able to keep him in sight, almost all the way down to the harbour, but that's where I lost him.

It was hopeless. I just couldn't keep up. My body was completely worn out. And he was fast—as fast as I used to be.

I stopped, doubled over, trying to catch my breath, and trying desperately to make sense of what I'd just seen.

15 FEBRUARY

320 days to go . . .

Internet café

11:11 am

I took a seat right down the back, choosing a computer with its screen facing the back wall, away from prying eyes, although the place was practically empty.

I went straight to my blog. My shadowed profile pic appeared and I was reminded of the kid I'd seen at the courts yesterday. I was going crazy trying to work out why there was this guy running around the city who looked exactly the same as me. He must have been asking himself the same question.

But I couldn't waste any more time on that mystery just now—I had other important things to do.

I had a lot of messages on my wall. Some of it was horrible—complete strangers calling me all sorts of names. Some were from people who said they wanted to join my gang.

Like I was some sort of street gangster.

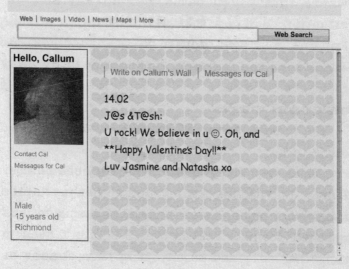

Web | Images | Video | News | Maps | More ⌄

Web Search

Hello, Callum

Contact Cal

Messages for Cal

Male
15 years old
Richmond

Write on Callum's Wall | Messages for Cal

14.02

J@s &T@sh:

U rock! We believe in u ☺. Oh, and

Happy Valentine's Day!!

Luv Jasmine and Natasha xo

Yesterday was Valentine's Day? I hadn't even noticed. At least it meant that I'd made it through the first half of the month.

'You're checking up on the psycho kid, are ya?'

Startled, I turned around towards the voice that had interrupted me. It was the man who ran the place—a tall, lanky guy in his mid-forties. He must have been bored with the quiet day. I couldn't blame him, but I wasn't up for small talk. I hit the 'close' button fast.

'Hey, I was just reading that,' he said.

'Oh, sorry, I have to get going,' I mumbled.

'He's got some hide putting himself up on the web like that,' the guy continued. 'I read somewhere that psychopaths will do anything for attention. But boy, that kid must be an animal. Imagine your own brother doing that to you.' He shook his head and then flicked a dead fly away from the keyboard beside me. 'No wonder his mum's lost the plot.'

He looked down at me and frowned. 'You come in here a bit, don't you?'

'Yeah, you've probably seen me here before,' I lied. 'I'm waiting for my dad to get my laptop fixed.' I turned back to face the screen and reached down to grab my bag. I hadn't been in there before. I had to get out of there before he worked out why I looked familiar.

'You kids these days, you have it too easy. Gadgets, mobile phones, chat rooms, all kinds of information you can download in seconds, fancy cars the minute you can drive. You don't have to work for anything,' he said, looking around at his empty seats and idle screens. 'Not like I had to. Too damn easy. You kids don't know anything about how hard life really is.'

Try living in a drain, pal, I longed to say.

'You're probably right,' I said instead. And with that, I got up and left.

16 FEBRUARY

319 days to go . . .

Burger Barn

12:05 pm

Boges and I were meeting in a busy, noisy fast-food place. We'd decided that it'd be safer than the drain, where two people caught lurking would surely mean questions and, ultimately, trouble.

Plus, I was thinking that making Boges come to the St Johns dump was bad enough. I really didn't want him to see the state of my latest living quarters.

I'd noticed the man from the internet café who'd spoken to me yesterday, but I kept my head turned as he passed.

Boges appeared, pulled out the opposite chair and plonked his tray down on the table. 'So what ya got for *me*?' he asked as he unloaded a couple of burgers, some chips and drinks.

'I saw this guy who looks exactly like me,'

I said in a rush. I waited for him to sit down, then I leaned in closer. 'I mean *exactly* like me. He was staring at me through the fence down at the Central Station basketball courts, and then as soon as I tried to talk to him, he bolted.'

'I don't blame him,' said Boges. 'If I didn't know you, I'd run, too. Dude, you look feral.'

I looked past my friend's head and shoulders to the frosted glass behind him where I could see my reflection. I had to admit that I did look like the sort of guy that any normal person would run away from.

'But Boges,' I persisted, 'I'm telling you, he was the spitting image of me. Exactly. The. Same,' I said slowly to push the point. 'And he was staring at me, like he knew me, or like he was wondering what I was wondering—why is there a guy in front of me who looks exactly the same as me?'

'You mean he had a bad fake tat on his neck, a bunch of piercings and hair like a rat's nest?'

'No.'

'So he *didn't* look exactly like you.'

'He looked exactly like I *used* to look,' I said impatiently. 'It was crazy. I was completely freaked out. We both were.'

Boges took a huge mouthful of his burger. 'You know that they say that everyone has a double—a *doppelganger*—and it's not a good sign if you run into yours . . .'

'What do you mean?'

'Let's just say it means bad news. Maybe it's just another of the mysteries of the city. I've been working on one of them—the DMO—'

'The what?' I asked.

'The DMO,' he repeated, pronouncing it like *Dee-mo*. 'The Dangerous Mystery of the Ormonds.' Boges grinned. 'I found out more about the riddle of the Sphinx—it's connected to a different sphinx to the one your dad drew.'

The only one I knew of was the one he'd drawn—the Great Sphinx of Giza, in Egypt.

'This other sphinx is very different,' Boges continued. 'She was some kind of psycho woman who was half lion. She had attitude—the sort of sphinx who stopped people passing by and asked them to solve a riddle, and if they didn't get it right, she'd kill them. Strangle and devour them.'

'OK, so what about the Roman guy? Where do you think he fits in?'

Boges shrugged. 'I'm still working on that. In History I asked Mr Addicot about whether there were any Roman connections with the Sphinx, and apparently Julius Caesar was involved in some business in Egypt around 48 BC.'

'This is the *Egyptian* Sphinx you're talking about now, right? Not cat-woman?'

'Right. We've got to keep in mind that the drawings don't actually mean exactly what's in them—we've gotta learn how to think like your dad did. Sort of diagonally. Sideways thinking.' Boges demonstrated his point with his hands. 'So, here's what I reckon he was trying to tell us: this huge secret he was in the process of uncovering is something to do with *history*, a life-and-death riddle and someone in power—a king or a ruler, someone like Julius Caesar.' He sat back. 'And then there's also something to do with a jewel—something you wear—that may or may not have been stolen from your dad's suitcase, and a blackjack . . . or a 21 . . . It's a bit lame, but it's the best I can do right now.'

I threw a chip at him. 'Someone in power. That really narrows it down. There's only been about a trillion kings and rulers in history.'

Boges picked the chip off his shirt and ate it. 'It could also just mean that your dad was stressing that discovering the truth about the Ormond Singularity was really important.'

'That part I do get,' I said, thinking again of the demented guy yelling out his warning on that hot December afternoon when it all began.

I sighed. Dad was certainly hiding things well. Putting the 'M' into the DMO.

'The only other thing we can do at this stage,' said Boges, 'is call that Eric guy from your dad's work and see if he knows anything at all about this from his time in Ireland—without giving too much away, of course.'

I took another bite of my fast-diminishing hamburger. 'Yep, I'll do that as soon as I can. Any luck on the words of the Ormond Riddle?'

'No, nothing's showing up.'

Nothing was making enough sense to me to matter. And I couldn't stop thinking about my double. It wasn't a surprise that it meant bad news.

'So what else has been happening?' I asked. 'Anything from school? Any special valentines from Maddy?'

'No,' Boges laughed. 'Maybe next year . . . You never know. All the guys at school are wondering where you are and what's happened to you. They're always asking me.'

It felt weird to know that everyone was talking about me.

'Mr Addicot asked me more about you, too,' said Boges, 'like trying to suss out whether I knew anything about your whereabouts. I just played dumb.' Boges grinned. 'Believe me, my friend, playing dumb was hard. Very hard. Especially when I've been busting my brain applying for a scholarship to the robotics lab of the University of Pennsylvania.'

'Pennsylvania, USA?'

'Uh-huh. Their research lab's been awarded millions of dollars in grants to develop robotic cockroaches.'

I gave him a kick under the table. 'Weren't the cockroaches at my dump good enough for you?'

'Hey!' He kicked me back.

Boges had finished eating his hamburger and was eyeing mine. 'Hands off!' I ordered. I pulled out my mobile phone and found the picture of the red-head I'd taken when I was perched up the tree.

'This is who grabbed me off the street that night near Memorial Park,' I said. 'I tracked down the house they took me to. Somehow, we have to find out who she is.'

Boges snatched the phone from me, his expression startled. 'How did you take this?'

'Through an open window. I was up a tree at the time. I tried to zoom in as much as I could, but, you know, this phone isn't that great. And, anyway,' I said impatiently, 'who is it? You know her?'

'This chick was on the news last night. I'm sure of it.'

'So who is she?' I asked, hoping to find out how I seemed to recognise her without actually seeing her.

'You're up a tree, taking photos of this woman through a window while I'm watching the exact same person on TV? Man that is *weird*!'

TV? I was starting to get annoyed at Boges, stringing me along, and I was about to tell him so when he finally said, 'This woman is none other than Oriana de la Force, "the flame-haired leading criminal lawyer in the city", as the journalist on the news described her . . .'

Criminal lawyer?

'Is *this* the woman you think abducted you?'

'You really know who it is?'

He rolled his eyes at me. 'I'm about ninety-nine per cent sure it's the same woman. I was watching this show last night, and the journalist said that Oriana—this woman,' he said, shoving her picture in my face, 'is notorious for taking on difficult and dangerous clients.'

I must have recognised her distinctive voice from seeing her on the news myself! '*She's* difficult and dangerous!' I said, with a half-laugh, thinking about the way she pushed me around and screamed at me the night I was abducted.

'I saw it on TV last night—a current affairs programme,' continued Boges. 'But, anyway, that wasn't the first time I'd heard of her. Cal, anyone who takes an interest in what's happening in the world, or at least in the city, would know about her.'

It was true I didn't take much notice of the news, although being on the run had changed that. Being part *of* the news, making headlines, had forced me to take an interest.

'But why would a leading criminal lawyer become involved in a kidnapping?'

'If you were going to commit a major crime, being a criminal lawyer would have to be a huge advantage, right?'

'I guess it wouldn't be the first time a *criminal* lawyer has given a new meaning to their title,' I added.

'Exactly, and a criminal lawyer would know all the traps, and Oriana would know better than anyone how to avoid them. So either she saw your photograph in the newspaper and wanted to adopt a lovely teen male just like you—'

I glared at him.

'Or,' he continued, 'she, herself, or a client of hers, is also after the Ormond secret. The DMO!'

Oriana de la Force had made it very clear that the fortune Dad had hinted at in his letter

84

to me was partly known to her. Too many people knew about it. Had he given too much away when he delivered his paper at the conference? The dangerous mystery of the Ormonds . . . How the hell was I supposed to compete against a brilliant lawyer like Oriana—a lawyer who would easily toss a kid off a cliff? And how could I stay alive when a criminal like Sligo, with all his wealth and underground connections, wanted me dead? I was just an ordinary kid! Well maybe not ordinary any more—but how was *I* going to win against these people? Luckily Oriana, at least, figured it was better to keep me alive. But for how long?

'You know,' said Boges, 'I've never heard of anyone who's had so many people after him—the cops, the infamous king of the underworld, a leading criminal lawyer—plus, and I know you hate hearing it, your own family think you're some kind of monster. It's messed up.'

I looked up from checking the time on my phone to see Boges's eyes huge in his frozen face. 'Don't move,' he hissed through gritted teeth. 'Don't even think about turning round.'

Without moving his lips, Boges muttered, 'Your uncle and some other dude just sat down at the table behind you. Whatever you do, don't turn around.'

Rafe?! Frantic, I tried to think of a way through this. If Rafe spotted me, I was gone. Every instinct was saying *run!* I hunched down, trying to shrink.

Boges had also hunched down, hand to his head, as if he was thinking deeply. If Rafe spotted *him*, I'd be next. I slid down further in my seat.

The two men behind me were deep in conversation.

'I've given the matter a lot of thought,' I heard my uncle's voice behind me, barely above a whisper. 'It'll give her a sense of security that she won't ever have while the house is still in my name.'

'Have you thought about the implications of this?' said the other man. 'How are you going to protect your own interests?'

'It's Win's interests I'm thinking of.'

Win's interests. Rafe was talking about my mum!

'If she knew she had the house in her name, it would be a great load off her mind. She's already got a daughter in intensive care and a son . . . well, that kid hasn't had it easy, but the less said about him the better. She's in a terrible way. I'm willing to do anything to help her.'

'But signing over the house,' protested the

other man, 'that's being too generous. You're forgetting your own interests—your own security.'

'Listen, I can't expect you to understand. This is my brother's wife, *Tom's* wife, and family we're talking about. They're all I have. They're all I care about. I feel I have to do it.'

'I can tell you've made up your mind, Rafe. Very well. Come around to my office tomorrow and we'll do the paperwork.'

'I know Tom would have done the same for me. I mean, if I'd been in a similar situation.' There was a pause. 'This coffee is undrinkable,' he added.

A moment later, I heard the scrape of the men's chairs as they got up and left.

I let out a huge breath. I hadn't dared to breathe during that conversation. My mind was spinning. Rafe was signing over his mansion to my mum? I felt a mixed-up rush of gratitude and guilt.

'That was way too close! Did you hear all that?' I asked Boges when I could speak again.

He nodded. 'See? You've been way too hard on him, dude. His heart's in the right place. He's just got a seriously messed-up way of showing it.'

'You were right,' I said, still almost numb with shock.

Boges sat opposite me, scratching his head

like he was trying to put all the paranoid pieces together. He looked at me, waiting for me to say something.

'I think,' he continued, when it was clear I wasn't going to, 'he's been trying to hold everything together—to deal with everything alone.'

Just like me, I thought.

Stormwater drain

4:46 pm

There was no-one around as I slipped through the fence near the railway yards and made my way back towards the big stormwater culvert. The crickets stopped their chirping as I sneaked past them in the long grass.

My mind was still whirling from seeing Rafe earlier. I felt such confusion and guilt in my stomach.

I hurried down the sloping drain. I'd sleep here for a few more nights, I thought, and then go back to suss out the St Johns house.

18 FEBRUARY

317 days to go . . .

10:32 am

I sat up in the alcove in the drain, the drawings spread around while I stared at them by torch-light. I was trying to work out what the half-woman, half-lion sphinx might have meant. Had my dad been trying to warn me again about the dangerous woman he mentioned in his letter? The beastly, answer-demanding Oriana de la Force?

The sounds of the city echoed through the drain, and my mind began replaying the moment I'd turned and seen my double staring at me. Had he seen something in me that scared him? Maybe he also knew that seeing your doppel-ganger meant doom.

19 FEBRUARY

316 days to go . . .

Kendall Cove

8:07 am

I'd risked going for a swim off a rocky cove not far from Dolphin Point, a spot where people rarely swam because of the strong currents that often whirled around there. When I first dived into the water it was pretty calm. It felt so good and refreshing to be underwater and free, but I could also feel that the ocean was growing rougher by the minute.

It was a stinking hot day and as I floated on my back and looked up at the sky I saw that in the southwest, thunder heads were building— huge grey cauliflowers of cloud with ominous, flattened tops. Time to go.

I climbed up the rocks and hurried to my backpack, secured in a cave-like hole well above the high water mark.

I moved as fast as I could, knowing that I

needed to get back to the stormwater drain to grab my stuff before the downpour.

Just as the first heavy drops started to hit the hot black tar of the roads, I made it to the tunnel. The roads hissed and steam lifted like ghosts. It was going to be one of those storms that dumps thirty millimetres on the city in half an hour.

Stormwater drain

10:53 am

I climbed up into the alcove and took out the plastic folder with Dad's drawings. I forced my sleeping-bag into my backpack and wondered how I could best stow the drawings. I was thinking that maybe I should secure the folder on the outside of the backpack with bungee straps, when I heard voices echoing through the drain.

I grabbed my torch, jumped down from my alcove—my backpack and the drawings in one hand, torch in the other.

Now the voices were loud—there was a rough-ness and a nasty edge that I knew meant trouble. One guy in particular had a very ugly laugh. I hesitated, wondering for a moment whether I should try to leave by the main drain, running straight into them, or avoid them by going down one of the smaller tunnels.

It was too late. Three guys appeared, emerging from the main drain into the small clearing before the other two channels branched off. They looked surprised to see me. Their surprise quickly turned to aggression.

'What are you doing here?' asked the leader, a tall guy with his black hair slicked back, a scar running through his left eyebrow, and what looked like a permanent sneer on his narrow lips.

'Yeah, we rule the drains. Who do you think *you* are?' the other two echoed from each side of their slick leader. Generally rats ruled the drains, but I thought it wouldn't be a good idea to say that.

The other two guys were smaller than the first. The shorter, stout kid was dressed in military-style gear, while the other guy had a shaved head and was squeezed into tight black jeans and a striped singlet, like some sort of urban pirate. They stood there, snarling at me while my mind raced for a way to deal with this.

I knew this scenario too well. I'd faced it plenty of times in the schoolyard. A gang of guys looking for a fight. A fight that they can't lose—three against one.

'What's in that bag?' demanded Scarface, making a lunge for my backpack. I jumped back quickly, out of his reach.

'And what's in the folder? Give us a look!'

I knew this game, too. If I didn't give them what they wanted, they'd jump me and grab it anyway. If I *did* give them what they wanted, they'd jump me just the same. You can't always talk sense to bullies, Dad once told me.

'Give me that!' barked Scarface.

'No way,' I said, taking a step back, putting some distance between me and them, so I'd have more room to move.

'You'd better,' said the guy with the shaved head, taking a step towards me.

'Why don't you come here and get it!' I said, playing for time, my mind working furiously for a strategy. I needed to deal with the leader first. If I could get him down fast, the other two wouldn't be too hard to sort out. I heard Dad's voice in my head: 'Watch their hands, and you'll see the punch coming before it lands.'

'Come on,' I taunted, 'if you want it so bad, come and get it!'

I glared hard at Scarface, keeping his hands in my peripheral vision. I wasn't feeling anywhere near as tough as I sounded, but there was no way I was giving my backpack to these losers.

The threesome looked surprised at my attitude, and Scarface's neck and face flushed red, his hands moving fast into furious fists. I braced myself, muscles surging with adrenaline.

He swung at me and before he knew what hit him I'd doubled over and charged my head into his gut like a battering ram. I heard him grunt as he went flying backwards, hitting the deck hard.

I kept going, avoiding his flailing arms and legs as he scrambled to recover his balance and his wind. But I was already gone, leaving them all behind me, racing away towards the Y-intersection.

I threw myself into the left-hand branch.

Scarface's swearing and the shouted threats of the others thundered down the drains.

This drain was smaller and more sloped than the main one. As my feet pounded along, the enraged footsteps of the three in pursuit pounded even louder.

'C'mon! Dogs! Freddy! Get the little scumbag!' Scarface yelled to the other two.

I had no idea where I was heading. They were gaining but I could hear something else—a sound I couldn't identify. It wasn't the distant rumble of trains; it was something else.

I kept running. I was passing dark entrances

to other much smaller drains, on my left and right, but they were too small to climb into. Water was starting to trickle from these small drains and onto the floor of the one I was running through. I knew that a city the size of mine would have kilometres of drains beneath it, but I hadn't realised just how extensive this underworld was.

Soon I was splashing through ankle-deep water. But still the footsteps behind me persisted.

The rumbling was getting louder and I suddenly understood what it was. It was the accumulating sound of dozens of drains rattling under the surge of the water that was pouring down from the city's gutters! Smaller channels were emptying their contents into larger ones; the larger channels in turn sending cascades of water into the huge culvert system.

The water was now halfway up my calves and it was getting harder to run. The guys after me were finding it harder, too.

I was starting to worry. *Give up, you morons!* We all needed to get out of the drain. I remembered Dad telling me that fast-running water, once it gets over your knees, is far more dangerous than it seems.

The drain was becoming steeper, sloping down towards some place I didn't even know.

Even the strongest swimmer would find it hard to do battle with the combined tide of thousands of tonnes of water that were descending on the roads, footpaths, and freeways of the city. I was struggling to stay in control. The sound of rushing water echoed loudly throughout the drain and I couldn't tell whether I was being chased any more. All I could hear was the roar of the rising water.

Now I was in big trouble, being bumped along by the powerful surge of the fast-flowing water. It knocked me off my feet and I struggled to hold the folder with Dad's drawings and the torch up over my head to keep them dry. When a huge surge of water suddenly hit me, I lost my balance completely, and both the torch and the folder flew out of my hands.

As soon as the torch hit the water it went out, throwing me into total darkness. I yelled and struck out in the rising drain water, which carried me along like a bodysurfer. I blindly stretched out my arms and fingers, desperate to find the plastic folder. I was only thinking about the drawings.

The power of the surge was pushing me along faster than I could ever swim. It bumped and crashed me against the walls. I had no idea where the drawings were. I was screaming in the dark, hurtling along, shouting for help although there was no-one to hear me.

Ahead of me I thought I could see bluish light.

The light was getting stronger. Now I could see a grilled entrance above the chop of the ocean. The drawings were lost. By now they'd be somewhere off the coast, sinking to the bottom of the sea. And I could be joining them any moment.

The surge pushed me faster and faster towards the grille and the ocean. But then I saw something that I could scarcely believe. In front of the grille was a mesh screen, catching plastic and rubbish. And slap bang right in the middle was the folder! I crashed into it and grabbed the folder. The mesh screen busted out on the impact of my body, and flew down to the seething ocean below. I hung on to the sides of the grille with one hand, the folder in my other, while the gushing water tried to tear me down.

I clung there for a long time, my head barely above water, my fingers turning wrinkled and white, but I didn't let go of that grille or the folder.

After what felt like an eternity, the water began to subside. Eventually the water level dropped completely, putting my feet back onto the hard ground.

1:50 pm

Everything was soaked. The gang of three was long gone. I'd made my way back out of the drain and was now walking along unnoticed in the rain—just another drenched pedestrian, sodden and dripping.

I called Boges from a public phone, and he quickly came to my rescue . . . again. I don't know how, but he managed to fix my damaged mobile and torch, and he gave me some dry clothes and a waterproof bag to store things more safely.

After about ten minutes he had to go again. If only I could have followed him.

5:33 pm

The alcove in the drain was saturated. Puddles sat where I'd been sleeping—clearly it had not escaped the stormwater level. I tried to sweep it out with my wet clothes, so I could rest up for a bit, but I knew I couldn't stay much longer anyway and risk being trapped.

9:01 pm

I settled down, trying to sleep. My body and mind were still churning over the gang I'd faced and the flooding storm. I hated fighting.

Back in Year 1 at school, one day, Boges and

I were about to have our lunch on the benches under the trees when two big kids—Kyle Stubbs and Noah Smith—approached us.

'What's that rubbish you're eating, weirdo?' Kyle said, pointing at Boges's lunchbox.

'Yeah, weirdo?' echoed Noah.

Mrs Michalko had packed Boges fried potato dumplings. She'd put in extra because she knew I loved them, too.

Even at six, Boges was reasonable and logical. 'It's called *piroshki*, and you're the weirdo, not me.'

Kyle kicked Boges's lunchbox, sending the potato dumplings flying out everywhere.

They rolled and became coated in playground dust and grass.

'What'd you do that for?' asked Boges. 'What am I supposed to have for lunch now?'

'Oh, boohoo,' mocked Noah.

I looked around for a teacher but there was no-one in sight.

Kyle kicked at some of the piroshki on the ground. 'You can still eat this,' he said, with an ugly grin.

With his grubby hands, he scooped up some of the dirty potato dumplings. 'Come on, open your mouth!'

Noah grabbed Boges and tried to prise his

mouth open. Boges kicked and struggled, almost falling off the bench. I didn't know what to do; I was so much smaller than these guys. But when I saw Kyle trying to squash the dirt-encrusted piroshki into Boges's mouth, something like fire raced through my body. With all my strength, I flew off the bench where I'd been sitting, and rammed Kyle Stubbs. I was only small, and Kyle was huge, but he went flying, knocking Noah in the process to the ground with him.

'Come on, Boges!' I yelled, swinging round and yanking my friend up.

As Kyle and Noah tried to get back to their feet, we raced past them, kicking dirt into their faces.

They never bothered us again.

20 FEBRUARY

315 days to go . . .

10:31 am

'Can I please speak to Eric Blair?' I asked. I'd finally decided to call Dad's work to find out if Eric knew anything.

'I'm sorry,' replied the woman on the other end of the line, 'Eric Blair's on sick leave. He's . . . he's not well. I can take a message for you, but I'm afraid I'm not sure when he'll be returning to the office.'

'That's OK, I'll call back another time,' I said, hanging up.

Straight away my phone rang, taking me by surprise.

'Hello?'

'Why haven't you called me?'

'Winter?'

'Who else would it be? What's the deal? Why the silence?'

'What? I've been trying to call you—I tried you

heaps. Your mobile's been switched off for two weeks!' I realised how desperate I must have sounded and started to tone it down. 'Whatever.'

'Sometimes I'm hard to catch. There are things I have to do. Now, do you want to see that angel or not?'

Swann Street

11:29 pm

As I waited for Winter near the Swann Street station entrance, I looked over a community noticeboard at ads for part-time work, room-mates, sales of laptops, cars and furniture. I moved further into the shadows when I saw some 'no psycho' tags next to a curling Wanted poster with the face I once used to have on it.

Everyone seemed to want a piece of me.

I patted my backpack, checking to make sure the drawings were safe. I'd slipped the folder underneath the plastic backing of my bag, and unless someone did a really serious search, the drawings couldn't be seen.

11:35 pm

I spotted Winter before she saw me. In her drifty clothes, with the light of traffic headlights behind

WANTED

CALLUM ORMOND

Have you seen this youth?

DESCRIPTION

Age: 15 yrs old   Hair: Blond
Height: 178 cm   Eyes: Blue-green
Weight: 75 kg   Complexion: Medium

If you have any information regarding the
whereabouts of this wanted person, please
contact Police Crime Force Unit #5, immediately.

CAUTION

Do not approach. Suspect is considered armed
and dangerous.

her, she seemed like some strange being from a
spirit world. As she walked closer I could hear
the faint chiming of tiny silver bells that lined
the bottom of her long, white skirt.

To my surprise, she kept on walking past me.

'You wanna see the angel, don't you?' she said, turning back, raising one eyebrow.

I looked into her dark, almond-shaped eyes and she gave me one of her cool smiles.

'I could have waited until tomorrow,' I said, 'but you insisted it had to be tonight.'

'That's right. I'm busy tomorrow.'

'School?' I asked.

She shook her head. 'I don't go to school. I'm home-schooled. But it still had to be tonight. There's a full moon. I need that.'

'Are you planning on turning into a were-wolf?' I joked.

'You'll see. Well, come on then!'

Although I was joking about the werewolf thing, I realised as I followed her that I had no idea what she was up to. Boges's words of warning were all I could think of. Good cop, bad cop.

11:48 pm

I hurried along to keep up with her as she led me through the city streets, her wild hair trailing behind her. She walked like someone in charge of the world.

It wasn't until we came to the bottom of a hill that I recognised the lane leading off to Memorial Park. The park I was abducted from.

'Where are we going?' I asked.

'You'll see.'

'I'm the sort of guy who likes to know where he's going.'

'Are you now?' She paused. 'I thought you wanted to see the angel.'

'I do. I just wanna know where he is already.'

'Look, we'll get there quicker if you quit the questions.'

Memorial Park

11:52 pm

Last time I was here I ended up in a car boot, and then locked in a closet. I hung back.

'Come on!' Winter grabbed my arm. 'You're not afraid, are you?'

'Of course not,' I lied.

'Then come on. We're nearly there.'

She hurried along in the moonlight, silver bells ringing on her skirt. I tried to stay cool, but alert.

11:59 pm

I kept looking around me, checking out every movement in the shadows. In this dark and secluded place, anyone could ambush us—or *me*. My heart jumped at the thought and a sickening feeling in the pit of my stomach made it hard to concentrate. I was braced, ready for anything. To run like hell or fight for my life.

We stopped at the low, wide steps at the front of the cenotaph. I'd never been this far into the park before.

'Sometimes the homeless sleep in here,' Winter said, dragging open the rusted iron gates that had once closed off the central area of the memorial. The lock looked like it had long since flaked away.

Just before going in she turned and held out the watch on her wrist. 'See?' she joked. 'It's almost midnight, there's a full moon and I haven't turned into a werewolf.' She laughed and bared her teeth. 'Not yet, anyway.'

We stepped over scattered rubbish and leaves and I tried to relax as she took my hand and led me further into the moonlit interior.

21 FEBRUARY

314 days to go . . .

Cenotaph
Memorial Park

12:01 am

I found myself in the middle of a wide, circular space with an ornate mosaic floor. Ahead of me, a figure stood on a tall stone pedestal—the sort of statue you see on graves or memorials. It was almost like being back at Crookwood Cemetery, when Boges and I were looking for the Ormond mausoleum at midnight.

It had been a warm summer night, but now a cold wind had blown in, lifting the dead leaves, making them skitter in an eerie little whirl. I shivered then looked up at the ghostly statue.

'That's not an angel, it's just a soldier!' Fear gripped me tighter. I was trapped. I'd followed her willingly into this creepy joint and now anyone could grab me, or the drawings.

I was about to hurry back down the steps when she called out to me.

'Where are you going? Look up!'

She held out her arms and looked to the sky. 'There's your angel!'

I hesitated a moment, then did as she said. I lifted my eyes until I was looking right over the statue's head and at the stained glass windows high up the wall of the cenotaph. I gasped. There, lit by the light of the moon shining through the coloured glass, glowed the huge figure of the angel *exactly as my father had drawn him*! His gas mask slung around his neck and tin helmet on his head. Behind him were his outspread wings.

I was stunned. I had found the angel.

I don't know how long I stared at him. It wasn't until I lowered my gaze and found an inscription at the bottom of the figure that I

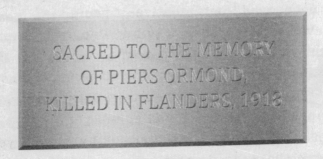

SACRED TO THE MEMORY
OF PIERS ORMOND,
KILLED IN FLANDERS, 1918

realised why Dad had drawn this angel twice—
first in his letter to me from Ireland, and again
from the hospital bed.

'Ormond.' I finally spoke. 'That's my surname.'
I turned to the girl beside me.

'I know that. And yet you didn't know about
this memorial?'

'I had no idea,' I said, pointing to the stained
glass window. 'Dad told me ages ago that a relative had died in the Great War but that didn't
really mean anything much to me. I think he
must've found something out about it when
he was in Ireland and—' I stopped myself in my
tracks; I'd been on the verge of telling her about
Dad's last letter from Ireland where he'd begun
explaining the massive discovery he was in the
process of uncovering.

'And?'

She frowned, realising I'd stopped myself for
a reason. 'It's not a very common name,' she
said. 'He could be a relative of yours.'

What did it mean? Why had Dad drawn Piers
Ormond? How did Winter know about it? My
excitement quickly changed to suspicion. 'So how
do you know about this angel? Where did you
find out about him? Did Sligo tell you?'

'Sligo?' Winter repeated. 'Why would you
think that? *He* doesn't know about this. *He's*

never been here.' She gestured towards the angel. 'This is where I come to get *away* from people like Sligo. Stop worrying, Cal. Your angel secret is safe with me.'

'What do you mean, *secret*? Why are you saying that? Why do you think there's some secret connected to the angel?'

In the moonlight I saw her roll her eyes.

'Oh man. Does being dumb come easy to you or do you really have to work at it? Of course there's a secret about the angel! Why else would you be so desperate to find out more? Why else would you be carrying drawings of this very angel around with you? Why would Sligo be chasing something called the *Ormond* Singularity? Of course there's a secret! You must think *I'm* stupid! Is that it?!'

She was right. It wouldn't have taken a genius to figure that out.

'I think you're a lot of things,' I said, finally, meaning that she was beautiful, strange, secretive, mysterious . . . and downright irritating, 'but *stupid* isn't one of them.'

She flashed a look at me. Now *she* was wary, unsure whether my answer was meant as a compliment or an insult. After a pause she spoke again. 'I've known about this angel almost as long as I can remember. I used to come here when I was little. When we were living in Dolphin Point. And then after the accident I came back here a lot.'

'The accident,' I asked, 'when you lost your parents?'

She didn't answer me. I knew her parents had died in an accident, but what exactly had happened? It was probably still far too soon for her to reveal that to me, if ever. She turned away to look up at the angel again. 'Yeah, I used to come here all the time. This was my special spot. It's cool in here in the hot weather, and during the day it's mostly deserted. I still like to sit here sometimes, especially when I'm sad.'

If I hadn't seen the sadness on her face when she showed me the photographs of her parents in her locket, I would have said that Winter Frey was way too cool for sad.

Too cool and too tough.

I started to feel that just maybe I could trust her. Was she telling the truth? I had no way of knowing. I put Boges's warnings to the back of my mind and tried to enjoy the moment. This angel finally connected the Ormond name with two of my dad's drawings, and to the Ormond Riddle. This stained glass window with its information about Piers Ormond was a huge piece of the puzzle Boges and I were trying to put together. I whipped out my mobile, took a picture and sent it to Boges.

It suddenly darkened. A cloud must have hidden the moon. I turned around to thank Winter for showing me the angel. But she was nowhere to be seen. While I was photographing the angel and sending it to Boges, she'd slipped away.

I could only hope she wasn't running straight to Sligo.

12:34 am

Liberty Square was quiet now. There were only a few people still on the streets. I was striding fast, my hood and collar pulled up around my face. I wanted to go back to St Johns Street to check out the derelict house. I couldn't go back to sleep in the stormwater drain. Not tonight.

Hideout
38 St Johns Street

1:30 am

I'd crawled under the house but stopped when I heard voices and someone moving around.

I crept up to the verandah and snuck around the side of the house so I could peer through a crack in a boarded-up window.

Three people sat around drinking on the floor, the floor where I had spent so many hard nights. Two men in shabby clothes and a younger woman with a gaunt face and stringy hair were sitting on my chairs, at my table. It was a hot night, but the woman was wearing long black mittens and had an old woollen shawl draped around her shoulders. They'd been through some of my food—there were empty tins rolling around. I didn't dare interrupt. I didn't want to stir up trouble. But I was really hungry and when I checked my pockets for money, I found I had hardly anything left of the money Boges had last given me.

I would have to find somewhere else to sleep.

2:01 am

I walked on, head down, and passed a loud group of people eating in one of those cosy twenty-four-hour cafés. I was so hungry and wondered for a moment how they'd react if I just walked on up to their table, sat down and started nodding and laughing along with them while helping myself to a big handful of their hot chips.

I was sure it wouldn't go down well.

And how would the waiter react if I sat by the

table next to them and started reading through the menu?

I knew that wouldn't go down well either. The problem wasn't just that I didn't have enough money. I looked a mess. I badly needed a shower, my clothes were dirty, I knew I must have stunk. I remembered reading about the Vikings and how when somebody did something really bad, their forehead was branded with a wolf's head and they were declared an outlaw—no longer part of the human community. No-one was allowed to give them food or shelter, or basically have anything to do with them. My grubby clothes, dirty face and hair were my wolf's mark.

2:32 am

I huddled in the corner of an open-sided shed in the disused railway yards and tried to direct my attention away from my dark and defenceless position, and my rumbling stomach, and on to the new lead with the angel.

3:13 am

It was raining. I dragged a few sheets of rusting corrugated iron and leaned them against the poles that held up the shed. They stopped some of the driving rain hitting me. I pulled my sleeping-bag up tight and tried to keep dry. The roar of the trains under the wind and rain kept me awake for a long time, until finally I fell asleep, too tired to care.

5:59 am

I sat up, sore from lying on the hard ground. The recurring nightmare had shaken me from sleep once again. The white toy dog and the screaming child and the crushing weight of desolation . . . Why was this plaguing me?

My sleeping-bag was soaked. My right shoulder was still aching and swollen, it just wasn't healing. I hoped it wasn't infected.

I got up and rolled the sleeping-bag up and left it tucked into the corner of the shed. I'd only managed a couple of hours' sleep but had to get moving.

6:23 am

The sky was lightening and a few people were moving around the city streets already. I walked quite a distance from the railway yards and found myself in an alley where a shopkeeper was unloading fruit and vegetables from the back of a van. He vanished inside the shop wheeling an upright trolley and deftly pulled the roller down with his foot, leaving a box of grapes sitting outside on the footpath.

When I was in Year 1, I pinched Tommy Garibaldi's aeroplane sharpener when he wasn't looking. He was the kind of kid that always came to school with the coolest, newest things that everyone else wanted. Before I took it I figured he wouldn't even miss it, but I felt so bad about it afterwards that I snuck back into class during break to put it back in his pencil case. I hadn't pinched anything since then. But now I had no hesitation. I scooped up the box of grapes and ran.

I stopped running when I reached a small park. Lorikeets were squabbling in the trees above me and I sat down near a big gum tree, ripped the lid off the box and pounced on those grapes. I devoured them like a pig at a trough, and before long I lay back on the grass, filled to busting point.

8:00 am

I was in real trouble. Nearly doubled over with cramps in my stomach. Maybe the van guy'd left the grapes out on the street for a reason.

Served me right for stealing them, I guessed.

I cursed the crowd of school kids in the

distance hanging around the bus stop making jokes and talking while I rolled around alone under some tree in some park in some neighbourhood in absolute agony.

How would my mum feel if she knew her kid was lying in a park, sick as?

Eventually the cramping eased up and I dragged myself further under some bushes where I couldn't be seen, and slept.

11:48 am

I jumped awake. Something rustled in the bushes around me. I kept still and listened carefully before turning to look.

'Yeah, it's a man in there.'

'Shhh, he's waking up.'

'I'll get him with this one. Watch this!' said another voice.

A stone flew through a gap in the bushes and hit the back of my head.

'Bullseye! Take that, bum!'

I could hear the slapping sound of high-fives. Slowly I turned my head and saw three pairs of small, shiny, black school shoes. I didn't care who saw me, I was furious. How could they think it was OK to treat me, another human being, like that? I leapt to my feet, emerging upright out of the bushes like a beast.

'GRRRRRR!'

They instantly ran like hell, screaming.

'This could be you one day!' I yelled out to them.

I stood there in shock, shaking my head, as they quickly disappeared. I thought again of the wolf's mark. So many people in the city wandered around wearing it.

11:53 am

My mobile was ringing somewhere back in the bushes and I scrambled to find it. 'Hello?' I asked, not recognising the phone number. Bright sunlight streamed down and sweat from the heat of the day and my anger poured off me. I moved into the shade.

'Is that Callum Ormond?' a woman asked.

Jennifer Smith? The mystery woman?

'Yes?' I said, cautiously, looking around me. There was only one little girl on a swing with her mum on the other side of the park.

'What happened last time we were supposed to meet? You said you were going to be there.'

She sounded genuinely concerned, rather than irritated, and I started to relax a bit—I'd have to stay on guard, but this was definitely not the voice of Oriana de la Force.

'I was on my way there,' I said, 'when something unexpected came up.'

That was true enough. I wasn't sure how much to say to her. I really didn't know who this woman was.

'Look,' I added, 'I thought you'd set me up. How can I know it's OK to trust you?'

I could hear her breathing on the other end of the line. I hoped she wasn't trying to find just the right lie to deliver to me.

'I don't know what I can tell you, Cal. I just know that your father had such big, warm, honest eyes, even in the midst of his devastating illness. He really wanted me to reach out to you. I put the photo he had of you in his wallet by the side of his bed—the one of the two of you by the car at the airfield, standing there with matching grins—and I held his hand and promised him I'd do whatever I could to help.'

I knew exactly which photo she was talking about. It was taken at air cadets, not that long before he left for Ireland.

'So what do you want to see me about?' I asked. 'Did you see Dad's drawings from his time at the hospice?'

'I did,' she said, and I believed her. 'But we can talk about that when we meet.'

'Did he ever say anything about something called the Ormond Singularity?'

'I don't think so. He was so sick by the time he came to the hospice. He was very difficult to understand sometimes.'

'You said you had something for me?' I said, recalling our earlier discussion. 'What is it?'

'I don't want to talk about it over the phone.'

I could hear the fear in her voice.

'I'll explain when I meet you, Cal. I know this is a dangerous situation. I know it is not easy for you, but it's not easy for me either.'

'So where are you thinking?' I asked.

'I'm working at the zoo at the moment and I think it will probably be safe for both of us if we meet there. I can answer all your questions then.'

'OK. When?'

'Sunday, the 28th?'

It would have to do. I'd have to wait.

'What time?' I asked, impatient to meet her.

'4:30? I'll be finished up by then.'

'Whereabouts?'

'Do you know the sundial?'

I did. It was a famous meeting point at the zoo. 'I'll be there,' I said.

She hung up and I put my mobile away. This woman had *known* Dad—had *seen* the drawings. I could feel hope returning. Maybe she'd helped

Dr Edmundson clear out Dad's stuff. What did she have for me? My pulse was racing with excitement.

With every new piece of information, my dad's secret was coming just that little bit closer . . . Despite the weakness my stomach cramps had left me with, and the fury I'd felt earlier from the stone-throwing brats, in that moment I felt like I could deal with anything.

12:26 pm

My mobile rang again and I snatched it up.

'I've just seen your pic of that angel! The Ormond Angel! Now we've got a real link to your family name,' said Boges. 'You've got to get into the country as soon as you can and talk to that old great-uncle of yours before he takes off for the great landing strip in the sky!'

'Yeah, you're right. Although he might have flown there already.'

'Not so, my man. He is still very much with us. Your mum mentioned him last time I saw her. She'd already contacted him, hoping you'd turned up there.'

'Then it's just as well I didn't.'

'This Ormond Angel breakthrough is really something. However . . .'

I knew he was thinking of saying something about not trusting Winter. I didn't want to hear it. Yeah, she'd done another disappearing act after the big reveal, but I didn't care. I wasn't going to tell him that.

'So did you already know about this Piers dude?' Boges asked.

'Dad mentioned some relative of his, ages ago—a great-great-uncle or a distant cousin or something—who'd died in World War I. This must be him. You mightn't be able to see the inscription beneath the window in the photo I sent you, but it says he was killed in 1918.'

Boges whistled down the line. 'Your dad must have found out about the stained glass window when he was in Ireland. But by the time he came back, he was too sick to follow it up. Or explain what it means for the DMO.'

'So he drew the angel,' I said, almost thinking aloud, 'and enclosed the drawing with that letter he wrote me. He *did* say he'd explain what it was about when he got home. He probably couldn't wait to get back and check the memorial out, but he never got that chance. He drew it a second time—' I said.

'Because it's really important,' Boges interrupted. 'I told you that already.'

I could hear the excitement in his voice. 'I'll

go and research this Piers Ormond guy. If he was important enough to have the stained glass window dedicated to him, he must be important enough to have earned a mention somewhere else.'

'Boges,' I said, changing the subject, 'I'm meeting the mystery woman on the 28th. The nurse who knew Dad.'

'Jennifer Smith; I know who you're talking about. How can you trust her after last time? You were pretty sure she'd set you up. She promised to deliver and then you were grabbed.'

'I know she's not Oriana de la Force, if that's what you're thinking. She talked about Dad in a way only an honest person could. And besides, I did all right last night—Winter Frey delivered the goods, and now we both know about Piers Ormond.'

'I'm sorry, buddy, but I still don't like the sound of her. You be careful. How do we know she hasn't gone running straight back to Sligo?'

'She's known about that angel since she was a little kid. And as far as we know, she hasn't told him about it. Otherwise he'd have recognised the angel when he saw the drawing. Besides,' I said, 'she doesn't even like Sligo. I don't think she's interested in helping him.'

'That's what she says.'

I pictured Winter and her intense, dark eyes and the way she looked at me so confidently, as if she had nothing to fear from me.

But Boges was right. I couldn't know for sure.

'So when can I see that angel?' Boges asked. 'I can't wait to get a decent look at it.'

'Tomorrow? Around 12:30?'

'Cool.'

The little girl who'd been on the swing at the other end of the park leapt off the seat and ran to her mum in a way that reminded me of Gabbi.

'Boges, how's Gabbi?'

'Sorry, my man, there's no news, but she's still hanging on like a real fighter.'

My jaw tightened—I had to be strong for Gabbi's sake. I couldn't help but think of all the times I'd made her cry when she'd annoyed me. I used to run away from her and hide and she wouldn't know where I was, and she'd fall in a heap on the floor and wail, thinking she'd been left all alone. I wished like anything that I'd been a better brother to her.

I was determined to somehow sneak into the intensive care ward and see her.

'And Mum?' I asked.

'She called into our place again last night. I told her that I still didn't know where you were. That was the truth—I didn't know. You could have been anywhere.'

'Did she look all right?'

'She's really thin, and still kinda unfocused. She's not great, dude, but she's just about moved out of your place now. Rafe's around there most of the time, helping her pack up the house.'

My reaction to hearing about Rafe was so different from just a couple of weeks ago. At least now I knew he had good intentions, and would take care of Mum. I'd hoped that having the house in her name might have cheered her up.

'There's been a tough-looking guy hanging round my place,' continued Boges. 'Wears a red singlet. He's tried to follow me a couple of times, too.'

'Red singlet? With a Chinese symbol on it?'

'You know him too?'

'Boges, you're gonna have to be even more careful than ever—he's one of Sligo's gorillas. Please make sure you're never followed by him. If he gets hold of me, I'm a goner. Last time he had me he was shoving me into the oil tank.'

'See? I told you that Winter Frey couldn't be trusted,' said Boges.

'Huh? What's she got to do with it?'

'She's part of the Sligo attempted murder club, dude. None of them have a conscience.'

'If she'd betrayed me,' I said, 'Red Singlet

would already know where I was and not be
hanging round your place trying to get a lead.'

Boges grunted. He knew I had a point.

22 FEBRUARY

313 days to go . . .

Cenotaph
Memorial Park

12:23 pm

Boges was already at the cenotaph when I arrived. He was standing there, staring up at the angel, completely blown away.

'That is an awesome angel!' he said without taking his eyes off it. 'It's just like your dad drew.'

We stood together in the cool interior of the cenotaph. The bright sun shone brilliantly through the stained glass angel, lighting the cement floor below with patches of colour—yellow and blue, red and green. We squinted our eyes and read the dedication to the fallen soldier.

Boges put his sunglasses on. 'There's something small beneath the gas mask. Something green and gold. Remember we thought that there was some sort of medal in your dad's drawing?'

'Yeah,' I said, pulling the angel drawing out of the folder. 'You can just make out an oval shape beneath the gas mask in the drawings as well.'

'This guy was really unlucky,' said Boges, 'to be killed in the last year of the Great War.'

'*Unlucky* seems to be something my family does well.'

'If we follow the clues your dad left for us,' Boges tapped the drawings, 'the luck of the Ormonds will change for the better.'

'I hope so, Boges.' *An astounding discovery*, my dad had said. Surely that would mean change for the better.

12:48 pm

'Thanks for keeping an eye on my family,' I said as Boges was leaving.

'Aw, it's nothing. Your mum says she likes me visiting. She says that seeing me makes things feel more normal. You know, sometimes she is almost like her old self. You kind of see that knowing sparkle in her eye, but just as quickly as it appears, it disappears again.'

Boges started scratching his head. 'I got here today by sneaking over Mrs Sadler's back fence instead of walking out the front door. Don't know how long it will take for them to wake up to me.'

Boges gave me his lunch and his money for the school excursion that day—a repeat visit to the observatory. Boges didn't need an excursion as an excuse to go there.

'Today I'd rather go to the library for free,' he said, 'and start digging around for information about Piers Ormond.'

'Why did they call it *the great war*?'

'There'd never been anything like it.'

Boges jumped back suddenly from the rusty gates.

'What is it?'

He grabbed me and dragged me back inside. 'Don't look now but see that guy near the entrance to the park? I'm sure he's the guy from the car that's been scoping my place.'

'Who? Red Singlet?'

'No, someone else. I wasn't sure if I was just being paranoid about this guy when I spotted him outside my house, but I think it'd be a little too much of a coincidence to run into him here in the park. He must have followed me.' Boges started scratching his head again. 'I thought I was careful. I'm so sorry, dude.'

'Forget it. We'll figure a way around this.'

I took a quick look and sure enough, there was a big guy lurking outside wearing a dark suit jacket over a T-shirt, black jeans, sneakers and sunglasses.

'If he comes over this way, he'll see you,' I said, looking round the edge of the cenotaph entrance. 'And he's got the place stitched up—there's no other way out of here.'

A tall iron fence with seriously sharp-looking, spear-like rails surrounded the park. There was no way anyone'd be able to get over that, let alone Boges.

I thought fast. 'It's *you* he's been told to follow,' I said. 'Chances are that even though he *thinks* he knows what I look like, I'm very different from how I look in the photos on TV and the papers.'

I pictured the clean-cut schoolboy photo on the police poster I'd seen while waiting for Winter the other night. I sure didn't look like that any more.

'I'll go straight up to him. That would be the last thing he'd expect a fugitive to do. I'll distract him while you go round behind him. By the time he works out he's lost you, it'll be too late.'

1:06 pm

'Got a light, mister?' I asked, sidling up to the big man.

'Disappear, kid,' he snarled from behind his wraparound sunglasses.

'How about a dollar then, mister?'

I was dimly aware of Boges making a wide arc around the park and heading for the entrance behind the big stooge who was scowling and trying to pretend I wasn't there.

'Come on,' I said, 'just one dollar. That's not much to ask from a guy like you, is it?'

'Get away from me!' He lunged at me but I was ready for him, and ducked out of his reach.

He tried to grab me again and this time I started running. I could see Boges slipping past behind him and out of the park, quickly vanishing up the lane and around the corner onto the main road.

The big stooge stopped coming after me and swore from a distance before turning around and heading towards the cenotaph building.

He had disappointment coming his way.

But then I saw him stop, turn back and look at me. He pointed at me, pulled out his mobile and then began walking away.

Internet café

1:23 pm

I tried to control my puffed-out breath before I stepped into an internet café. I wondered what the big man in the suit jacket was doing now.

He'd recognised me, I was pretty sure, and now he was probably letting Sligo know that I was in the area. I took a quick look around. The place was crowded but I found a free desk and chair and I logged on, all the time keeping a watch out of the window to the street. I'd have to move on quickly.

I knew there was a back door where the toilets were, so if anyone came in here after me, I could be out of the door and over the fence at the back in triple-quick time.

I pulled out one of Boges's sandwiches. Mrs Michalko had used some kind of sausage stuff I'd never eaten before, and I wolfed it down without thinking too much about it. As I had a look around the desk for a piece of scrap paper to make notes on, I found something that set my heart racing yet again . . . a sticker on the hard drive next to me with my face on it! It was like a smaller version of the poster I'd seen a few days ago, only it had some internet café alert, and something about my blog address, and a more recent picture of me from a security camera! I instantly shut my computer down and prepared for a hasty exit.

As I stood up from my chair and glanced around me I saw that the stickers were everywhere! On every computer! On the desks! On the walls! In front of every single person in there!

I was out of the back door and over the fence like a blur.

2:09 pm

How would I get information now? My picture was probably in every internet café in the city and the state! I didn't even get a chance to check my page.

📱 boges. my pic is all over internet café! NEW pic. must have taken it from security camera. just got out in time. didn't get any info. u?

📱 dude! that sucks. in library now. nothing 2 exciting on blog. let u know if anything changes. found the riddle the sphinx used on her victims . . . what goes on 4 legs, then 2 legs, then 3 legs?

📱 i give up.

📱 . . . a human being. first as a baby we crawl on 4 legs, then as adults we walk on 2. finally as old people we walk with a walking stick. 3 legs!'

📱 u reckon those numbers 4, 2 & 3 are clues to dad's puzzle?

📱 could be. don't forget the number 5 in the drawing of the old cupboard or door or whatever it is. that gives us 2, 3, 4 & 5. meaning?

📱 once I caught a fish alive.

📱 cal, ur hilarious. (i'm being sarcastic, in case u can't detect my tone by sms.)

5:13 pm

I'd been slowly making my way back towards St Johns Street, hoping that the place was empty. I'd have to wait until it was dark before actually trying to get in there. I wasn't looking forward to it, but was so happy to be heading away from the drain and the railway yards.

I kept my head down but occasionally I'd scan the people around me, wondering if I'd ever see that kid again—the one who looked exactly like me. Then I'd start to wonder whether I'd imagined the whole thing—seeing double, or something.

7:12 pm

I listened again on the verandah. All was still and quiet. Whoever had moved in, had moved out again.

I crawled up through the hole in the floor and collapsed. It was a strange feeling to be so relieved about being in this dump. Almost anything was better than the drain.

I had more room, a soft glow of candlelight,

my little radio playing softly and I'd found a tin
of beans I'd forgotten I'd hidden away.

📟 boges. i'm back at the mansion. b round any
time soon?

📟 i'll see what i can do in the next couple of
nights. hang tight.

26 FEBRUARY

309 days to go . . .

Hideout
38 St Johns Street

12:02 pm

'Sorry, dude, but I've only got a few minutes,' said Boges. 'I think Mum's getting suspicious. I don't *think* she would say anything to the police, but . . . she could slip up without meaning to. I don't want my charm to fade with the teachers at school, either. My grades are still up so they're pretty cool when I rock up to class late, or . . . not at all, but they could start seeing it as arrogance if I do it too much.'

He unloaded his backpack, tossed me a black cap, a charged phone battery, and then my new supplies: a bunch of bananas, a bag of bread rolls and more canned beans. He started laughing as he made a tower with the cans.

'What is it?' I asked, pulling the hat on.

'This diet of yours. It's primitive. Much more

of this,' he said as he added the last can to his tower, 'and you'll be swinging through the trees, jet propelled by natural gas!'

It was so good to laugh.

'You heard from that Sligo chick?' Boges asked.

'Winter. No.'

'Probably a good thing. Anyway I gotta go, but I'll keep you updated on your blog and let you know if I have any DMO strokes of genius—it's bound to happen, let's face it. And here,' he said, handing me two twenty-dollar notes, 'I fixed Mr Addicot's laptop for him. He gave me sixty bucks!'

'Thanks heaps.' If it wasn't for Boges I'd have been forced into handing myself in long ago.

'I know you'd do the same for me,' said Boges. 'Forget about it.'

27 FEBRUARY

308 days to go . . .

2:12 pm

I'd spent the whole morning in the library, but no-one had seemed to take much notice of me. Boges and I had both been trying to connect the numbers 2, 3, 4 and 5 to the range of clues we already had, but even his brain couldn't come up with anything. I went over all the connections we'd made in the drawings so far, but I couldn't get anything new. The Ormond Singularity remained as unfathomable as ever.

As I walked back from the library, I was starting to feel like I was just another face in the crowd. All I had to do was stay low and quiet and keep on the track of the dangerous mystery of the Ormonds. Maybe tomorrow Jennifer Smith'd give me the break I needed. It sounded easy. Somehow, I knew it wasn't going to be.

28 FEBRUARY

307 days to go . . .

Bus Depot

3:20 pm

It was hot and I was starting to get paranoid again about my appearance. I pulled my hat down low.

I was threading my way through the lines of people for the 3:30 bus to the zoo when I saw something that made me jump with fright. Red Singlet! What the hell was he doing here?

I immediately ducked into a doorway, peering around the edge of the corner to watch him.

He was showing a photo to people as they passed. I was sure that it was me he was asking about, and, after seeing the picture in the internet café, I was pretty sure he'd have something fairly up-to-date.

People walked on by, shaking their heads. They hadn't seen the psycho kid. It was clear Sligo had him there searching for me. Worse still, he was standing right next to the door of the zoo bus. I'd have to walk past him to get on board. I could hear the announcement saying the bus was about to depart. If I missed this one, I'd miss my meeting, and maybe my last chance.

Desperate, I searched for a way around him. I had to get on that bus. Something I'd thought about the other day flashed into my mind—a technique I'd read about called 'hiding in plain sight'. It required a lot of boldness and a simple prop, to make you practically invisible.

Now was my chance to see if it was actually true. Would it work? If it didn't, I was in big trouble. I knew what Sligo would do to me if he got hold of me again.

Keeping one eye firmly on Red Singlet, I edged over towards a very full rubbish bin. Beside it someone had dumped several cartons. I grabbed one of the cartons, quickly folded its lid down, put it on my shoulder as if it contained something, and with the cardboard hiding most of my face, I joined the queue getting on the bus, my heart thudding.

I could hear Red Singlet's voice from behind the cover.

'. . . considered very dangerous,' I heard him saying as I stepped past, so close he could have *touched* me.

'. . . I've been hired by the family to find him . . .' he continued as I stepped up to the bus, keeping the carton on my shoulder. The liar!

I glimpsed him turning away from my direction with the photo, so I quickly dropped the carton and edged into the bus as the driver was busy giving change to one of the passengers. I darted unnoticed into a seat at the back.

I slunk down as the bus pulled away from the kerb, and my hunter.

City Zoo

4:15 pm

I waited at the end of a small queue of people at the admission window, worried about the passing time. We'd arranged to meet at the sundial at 4:30. I still had fifteen minutes.

4:21 pm

When it was my turn at the admission window I was shocked at how expensive the entry fee was. I felt so stupid, but I'd guessed it was only going to be a few dollars. Like a kid, I showed the woman all the money I had—small change plus a ten-dollar note left over from the cash Boges had given me. I didn't have enough.

'Please,' I tried to explain, 'I'm only going to

meet someone at the sundial. I'm not going in to look at any animals. If you'd just let me in for this much?'

'You got a student card?'

'Um, no, not on me.'

Sure, here's my student card, I thought. *I'm Callum Ormond. 15 years old. Armed and dangerous. Let me into your damn zoo.*

'Look, I can't let you in unless you pay the full price. If I were to give discounts to everyone, the zoo would go broke. And then who would look after the animals?'

'Please,' I begged, 'I'm not asking you to do it for everyone, just for me. Just this once,' I argued, noticing the time on the wall clock behind her. If I hurried, I'd make it, but there was little time for delay. 'Please. It's almost the end of the day.'

Her face reddened. 'I don't make the rules! You should have arranged to meet somewhere else! That's the entry price!' She pointed to the amount on the sign above her window. 'And you haven't got it. End of story.'

She peered around me and gestured to the couple behind me in the line. I gathered up my money, shoved it back in my pocket and walked towards the gateway. Security guards were there taking people's tickets, one on each side of the gate. There was no way I could sneak through.

4:28 pm

If I failed to turn up a second time, no matter what excuse I came up with, it could have meant the end of my chance to speak to Jennifer Smith—the last link to my dad. I couldn't bear to lose her. There *had* to be a way in.

I walked away from the entrance area and turned down the road that ran alongside the zoo. There was no way I could climb over the tall metal fence that separated the grounds of the zoo from the road. I kept walking until I came to a turn in the road where a big tree grew hard against the fence. This was my last shot.

Hoisting myself up and trying to avoid the barbed wire running along the top of the wall was hard. I grabbed at the tree's branches with one hand and carefully placed my other hand underneath the barbed wire strands on top of the wall. I had to throw my hoodie across the barbs to give me some protection as I hauled myself over. I felt lucky that I'd done a lot of junior athletics—so many skills I never thought I'd need again in life were really coming in handy in this life on the run.

I threw my backpack into the bushes below,

near a few rocks and a small pool. I estimated the drop to be about four metres, so I slowly let myself down the wall so that I didn't have quite so far to fall. I landed hard and broke my fall as best I could, remembering to keep my legs relaxed and soft. I rolled over a few times before picking myself up and grabbing my backpack.

I took a quick look around and saw nothing but more bushes and the pool. It looked like I'd landed in one of the old, abandoned enclosures.

4:43 pm

Now all I had to do was find my way out of this enclosure, make it to the sundial, meet Jennifer and find out what she had for me.

I was late, but hopefully not too late.

Apart from a small grilled door in the wall behind me—and I didn't want to go in there in case I ran into a keeper—I couldn't see any way out unless I climbed up the rocky wall opposite me and pulled myself onto the wide footpath of the zoo above. There were people walking back and forth along there, but I was too busy making my way through the scrub to pay much attention to them.

I had just started climbing the rocks when I heard people calling out from above. This wasn't what I wanted—to be spotted by a whole bunch of people. I ducked down. People were yelling at me, pointing and shouting, but because they were all shouting together, I couldn't make out what they were actually saying. I pulled my mobile out and checked the time. I couldn't waste too much time hiding out down there in the bush. I needed to get to the sundial.

4:48 pm

I could see people pulling out their mobiles and taking photos of me! It would only be a matter of minutes before my identity was blown. Surely they hadn't recognised me from such a distance? Didn't they have better things to do? Like looking at the animals?

Just as I was about to turn all my attention into getting the hell out of there, without a care for who was watching, I saw something that first made my heart drop, then race like hell. Up there on the ground above, in the middle of the shouting crowd and grinning like a hyena, was Sligo's man, Red Singlet! He must have found someone who'd noticed me getting onto the bus earlier. I searched frantically for another way out.

It looked like I had only one option—trying my luck with that grilled feeding door I'd seen earlier in the wall.

The crowd was going crazy, as if I was some sort of wild animal myself. Maybe someone *had* recognised me, but all I could think of was Red Singlet and how to get away from him and to my meeting. I *had* to get to that meeting! And I had to shake him off somehow!

It was the tone of fear in the shouts from the crowds that made me finally take notice of what they were trying to tell me.

Slowly, the words penetrated my mind.

'Look out!' someone was calling. 'Get out of there! For God's sake get out of there! There's a—'

It was the last word I couldn't quite catch.

Cautiously, I stood up.

And that's when I saw him in front of me, mere metres away.

I froze and so did he, stopping dead in his tracks, raising his huge head higher to stare at me with merciless yellow eyes—a massive lion, golden brown with a black mane.

From a long way away came the sounds of the crowd that had gathered on the path above the lion's den and then I could no longer even hear that. I forgot about Red Singlet and the danger he represented. Every fibre, every cell in my body was concentrating on the huge beast standing before me, black-tufted tail swishing to and fro. The whole world seemed to be reduced to the two of us; that's all I could see, all I could focus on.

I felt adrenaline flood me with its icy strength—flight or fight. There was no way I could fight this animal; one thump from those great paws and my bones would be crushed. Flight was the only alternative and yet I knew that the minute I turned and ran, the massive predator would do the same. Four legs can outrun two legs any day.

Without taking my eyes from the huge beast, my heart beating hard, sweating all over, I started to back away, one foot after the other, trying to fix the lion where he was with my gaze, moving only my feet while I carefully retreated. I knew if I tried to climb back over the wall I'd come over, he would pull me down like a kitten pulling a piece of string. My only hope was making it to the door in the wall behind me. A sound like thunder made me jump and I was shocked at the power of his growl. His tail lashed faster, and he hunkered down, wriggling his hindquarters from side to side just like a cat about to spring at a bird.

I increased the speed of my retreat. This seemed to activate the lion. He gave a mighty roar and I knew he was about to jump on me.

I turned and ran to the grilled gate, trying to open it.

It wouldn't open!

From somewhere came the wailing of an alarm siren. That shocked me into realising that I was trying to open the door the wrong way. I wrenched it open! I raced through, but just as I slammed it shut behind me, something crashed against me, hitting my leg!

The lion's roar so close to my ear was deafening. I dared to turn round and saw to my horror that the huge beast had crashed right up against the gate. I prayed that it would hold fast under his massive bulk. He dropped down and stood there, glaring at me through the steel mesh, roaring with rage.

4:59 pm

I was in a small holding pen with another door at the other end. I raced through it into a wide corridor, away from the roaring lion. The alarm was deafeningly loud down there. Any moment, the place would be swarming with security. Red Singlet would be hot on my tracks. I had to get away! I was running down the corridor, past empty offices and laboratories, when I myself roared in pain. I looked down and was horrified to see a huge bloodstain seeping through the back of my jeans. Through the rip in the denim, I could see a deep gash, welling with blood. The lion's claw had got me!

Now that the shock was wearing off, my leg was becoming excruciatingly painful. I leaned against the wall for a second, feeling helpless and confused. Was it all over? I was trapped, just like the lion I'd faced a moment ago. I didn't know where to go and there was no-one I could turn to for help. The mobile pictures of me would be identified by now and making their way into TV news reports, police bulletins and newspapers. I'd completely screwed up my second meeting. Completely screwed up. But right now, I couldn't do a damn thing about it. I staggered into an empty room and collapsed into a chair, trembling all over.

5:10 pm

I seemed to be in some sort of storage area; under piles of cartons I could see old sinks with curved taps. Maybe this was one of the laboratories. I caught sight of a box from a pharmaceutical company, and peered at the label. Beneath a lengthy scientific name was a phrase which caught my eye—*pre-loaded tranquillising syringes*.

That's what I needed, I thought bitterly. A tranquilliser.

But the insistent sound of the alarm brought me to my senses. That wasn't the answer. I needed to stay alert and vigilant. I needed to remain at least one jump ahead of Sligo and Oriana de la Force. I needed to keep focused on escaping.

5:15 pm

I could hear voices approaching. I lurched over to the counter, picked up the box of syringes and stuffed them in a pocket on my bag. I looked around for some painkillers but found nothing.

I had to keep moving. And even though I felt like I couldn't move, I forced myself to keep going. I hoped Jennifer Smith would believe I wanted to see her.

I started down the corridor, ducking into another empty room when I heard voices.

The guy, a zoo official, started coming after me. I had no choice. Despite the pain in my leg, I made a sudden turn and ran back the way I'd come. Behind me, I heard him swearing and yelling into his two-way radio for reinforcements. Blood squelched in my trainers as I raced away.

At the other end of the corridor I found a locked door. Desperately, I looked around for another way of escape, ducking into an empty office to the right of the locked door. The

windows were also locked and the air condition-
ing was humming. I picked up a chair and acting
on instinct, I brought it down on the locked
window. Hoping to delay my pursuers a little
longer, I darted to the door of the office, slam-
ming it shut and locking it from the inside.
Avoiding the shattered glass, I threw my torn
hoodie over the jagged edges of the window
frame and hauled myself out of the window,
dropping to the ground about two metres below.
The jolt of the drop to the ground shot agonising
pain up through my leg.

I staggered to my feet and looked around. I
had landed on a narrow path between two buildings. Here, the sound from the alarm was a little
softer but I knew that the zoo would be crawling
with security and, by now, the police.

5:21 pm

The pain really hit me as I ran limping down the
narrow path past the other buildings. One of
the buildings nearby was a Portakabin with a
narrow verandah at the front where a line of
gumboots and workboots stood in an uneven row.
Hanging above them were several wet weather
jackets and coats. I limped up the two steps and
grabbed one of the dark green keeper jackets
and a pair of tall wellington boots. I hoped

they'd hide the blood that now soaked one leg of my jeans. I pulled my trainers off and pulled the boots on, wincing as I pushed my injured leg into one of them.

Awkwardly, I crept to the end of the verandah and peered around the corner of the building.

I could hear people talking as they headed towards the exit, fragments of conversations about what they'd seen in the lion's den.

'He can't have got very far,' I overheard.

Another voice answered: 'I've got him on my mobile. Take a look. That's him there in the grey hoodie.'

I pulled the dark green jacket closer around me with relief, and shoved my trainers into my backpack.

I slipped by groups of officials in khaki shorts with walkie-talkies, and clumped down the path towards the sundial, not even slowing to see if there was anyone there who could have been Jennifer Smith, past family groups with kids in pushchairs and a school group with their teacher. I was completely driven by fear, pain and the almost hopeless desire to escape unseen.

As quickly as I could, I hobbled down the path on legs that were shaking, blending in with the crowds who were already streaming towards the exit.

5:34 pm

I hobbled out of the entrance and onto the road within a group of senior kids from a rural school. I pretended to be part of the group, walking close to them, cowering beneath their happy chatter and teasing. No-one challenged me in my dark green jacket, or saw the pain of my leg on my face, although I got some stares because of my oversized boots. I kept scanning around for Red Singlet but couldn't see him.

My leg was throbbing and every step killed me. Would Jennifer ever trust me again? If I'd been alone, I probably would have fallen to the floor and bawled with pain and frustration.

5:52 pm

Hidden out in some bushland near the zoo, I raised my leg to stop the bleeding, and tried to rest and recover a little before finally wrapping it as best I could with a ripped-up shirt.

I peered out from my hiding place and saw that police had gathered over by the zoo entrance, which was now cordoned off with tape.

At least I was on this side of the tape.

I had no choice but to suck up the pain, look as above suspicion as possible, and join the short queue of people waiting for the last bus back to the city.

The rumbling of a helicopter thundered through the sky as the bus pulled away from the zoo, freeing me, for now, from capture.

Emergency Ward
Sacred Heart Hospital

7:05 pm

I quickly filled out a form, with a fake name, of course. Tom—for my dad—and Mitchell—the name of the first dog we had when I was little.

Maybe I was stupid to think that I could walk off the street and into a public hospital, but I felt far enough away from the attack at the zoo to be safe. Safe enough.

Or maybe it was because I'd lost a lot of blood and was light-headed. Too light-headed to think properly?

The bleeding had finally eased when I was called shortly after signing in by a doctor whose jeans I could see under the short white jacket she was wearing.

I sat up on one of the examination tables, while she cleaned out my wound, and gave me a shot of painkiller and stitched the injury. I noticed how she kept looking at the wound and frowning.

She went about her work in silence until it came time to give me another injection.

'Tell me again,' she said, 'about the big black dog.'

'Is that for rabies?' I asked, wincing at the sting.

'No,' she said. 'There's no rabies in Australia at the moment but animal bites can turn septic. Anyway, don't worry about that, just tell me more about that dog.'

I repeated my story of the big black dog. Except this time I made the story a bit more interesting, adding in a soccer ball I was kicking.

'You were kicking a soccer ball in those boots?'

'Stupid, hey?' I replied. *So stupid . . . Surely I could have come up with a more believable story.*

She secured the bandages with a clip and straightened up. 'You'll need to keep this dry. No baths or showers for the next three days.'

I assured her that wouldn't be a problem.

'These bandages will need changing in a day or two. I'll give you a letter for your GP.'

I nodded as she wrote up the GP's letter. Through the open doorway I saw a doctor on a phone, looking around quite tensely. He gestured to someone, and before I knew it, hospital Security had approached him. The police must have contacted them about me. I had to get out.

I stood up to leave as the doctor called me back.

'Tom,' she said, and I almost didn't respond at the unfamiliar name. 'I worked in Kenya for *Médecins sans Frontières*. I've seen those injuries before. That's not a dog's bite. Only the claws of a big cat make marks like that.'

'It wasn't a cat, it was a dog.'

'I'm not talking *domestic* cat.'

There was a silence while we stared at each other.

'Gotta go. Thanks,' I said, hurrying out of casualty and right past the doctor who had been talking to Security.

9:09 pm

I wandered around aimlessly in the dark, far from the hospital, my body aching with loneliness. It was more painful than my stitched-up leg. I thought again of the lion and his massive eyes, the way they stared coldly into mine . . . before he reached out and tore my leg open.

I saw something in those eyes that made me uneasy. I couldn't help but wonder if I would eventually crack and live up to the 'psycho kid' tag I'd been given. I was afraid that being trapped and isolated could do it. Maybe sooner rather than later.

I noticed a public phone across the street and was instantly drawn to it. I hobbled over to it and dialled Rafe's number. I couldn't use my mobile for fear of being traced.

'Hello?' came Rafe's voice down the crackly line.

I thought of him on the other end, with my dad's face.

'Who is this?' he said. 'Is that you, Cal?' he asked, his voice quickly warming. 'Look, son, please come home. Your mother needs you. We all need you.' He paused for a moment, waiting for me to say something, but I just couldn't.

'Are you still there?' he asked again. 'Say something, please?'

'Hi,' I finally whispered. It was all I could muster.

'Cal! You're OK! Please come home.'

'Cal?' he said again after a long silence.

'Who is it?' I heard Mum ask Rafe softly in the background.

But I'd hung up before anyone had a chance to say anything more.

9:38 pm

There was no way I'd hear from Jennifer again, I convinced myself. I'd been hoping she'd call me, ever since I left the zoo. Give me a chance to explain myself. Arrange to meet somewhere else, tonight. But who was I kidding? If she was going to call she would have done it by now. I'd have to go back to St Johns and rest up.

My mobile rang just as I'd given up on Jennifer Smith. I hoped it would be her. Or Boges.

'Cal, it's me. I have to see you.'

It was Winter. I imagined her with her dark, floaty hair and wondered where she was calling from.

'Hi,' I said, my image of her cloud of hair quickly transforming into the memory of her creeping around Sligo's car yard, stealing car parts. Was she fooling me, like she was fooling Sligo? Somehow, even in my uncertainty, my miserable mood lessened at the sound of her voice.

'I was thinking we could meet up at the Hibiscus Café. It's open pretty late. We could have a quick chat and a smoothie or something?'

'You know my situation,' I said, not wanting to say too much on the phone, 'money-wise.'

'Listen,' she said. 'You supply the company. I'll supply the cash. OK?' Then she giggled. 'That's not quite true. Sligo will supply the cash—although he doesn't know it.'

I smiled on hearing her giggle, but stopped myself.

'I saw you,' I blurted out, 'when you were in Sligo's car yard. You were crawling around looking into the cars and under the tarpaulins.'

'What are you talking about?'

'The car yard. The other day. I came to look for you, and I saw you there sneaking around.'

'You're wrong, Cal,' she said. 'Why would *I* have to sneak around Sligo's?'

Forget the cute giggle, I told myself. Remember Sligo. This girl hangs round with Sligo. This girl tells lies.

'Anyway,' she continued, back to her earlier, friendly tone, 'there's something I need to talk to you about. Something really important. Something very dangerous.'

'What is it?'

'I'll tell you when I see you. Where are you now?'

'I'm not that far from the Hibiscus Café. I'm just outside the—' I stopped. What the hell was I doing? Telling Winter Frey where I was? For all I knew, Red Singlet might have been standing right beside her, taking down notes.

'Never mind,' I said, thinking fast. I *did* want to see her. But I'd have to arrange some place to meet where I could set myself up earlier—somewhere I could check out her arrival, and see whether she'd come alone. Or not.

9

I thought of the clock tower near Liberty Square as the perfect spot for me to watch her. It had a great view of the east side of the mall where there was another café that I knew would be open.

'What about meeting at the Blue Note at ten?' I said. 'Hello?' I said, puzzled, when she didn't respond. The line must have dropped out. She was gone. I looked for her number to call back when the screeching of tyres made me jump.

A black Subaru had screamed to a halt, mounting the footpath only metres behind me! Red Singlet was already halfway out of the driver's seat!

And was there another person in the back seat? Someone with dark, floaty hair who'd just set me up?!

I turned and ran. I had to ignore the pain in my leg and I hared across the road, ducking stray cars, zigzagging to the other side, ignoring the blasts of horns and the curses of shocked and angry drivers. From the corner of my eye I could see Red Singlet coming after me. He was fast. He was ducking and weaving the same trail as I had.

I put my head down and raced like hell down the footpath, knocking people out of my way, crashing around corners.

And he kept right up behind me.

I was almost at the train station. I raced to get there, hoping that I could lose him amongst the late-night commuters and party-goers, going up and down the ramp to the dozens of platforms.

But a quick sideways twist of my head showed me that I was far from losing him. Red Singlet was making ground on me. He was closing the gap and he knew it. Now I could even see his evil grin as he strained to catch me. I'm right here behind you, he seemed to be saying. You're dead!

I forced my injured leg to keep working, racing along at a singeing pace. I knew only too well what would become of me if I were caught. Torture. Death. I had to outrun him.

Underground train line
Liberty Square

10:02 pm

I jumped and scrambled over the ticket barriers, then turned around to see if I was still being followed. I could see a railway attendant talking into his walkie-talkie and had no doubt he was reporting me. I kept running, my breathing coming hard, and the ache in my bad leg weakening me even further. But I couldn't stop now.

I ran down onto the first-level platform, hoping to jump on a train and free myself of my pursuer, but the train was pulling out too fast already.

More stairs led to lower platforms. I had no choice but to keep descending.

Red Singlet thundered behind me. In a panic, I made a bad move and jumped from about halfway down the stairs. I felt the stitches burst as soon as I landed.

I howled and stumbled with pain, my wound splitting open again, but somehow I kept going.

My backpack bumped hard and heavy on my shoulders as I hit more stairs. I wanted to throw it off me, but I couldn't. Everything important to me was in there.

Including a box of tranquillising syringes!

Still racing towards the trains going to who knows where, I kept going, reaching my hand back, feeling around for the pocket in the side of my backpack where I'd hurriedly stashed the syringes back at the zoo. My fingers closed around one of them and I pulled it out, checking it as I ran. The loaded syringe, with its cone-shaped lid over the sharp end, was enclosed in a sterile plastic sleeve. I tore it open with my teeth as I ran.

Tiring now, the blood starting to rush free from my leg, I was slowing down.

I saw Red Singlet come flying down the flight of stairs to the platform I was running along. Now he was at the bottom of the steps and still coming after me. Only a handful of people stood around, waiting, not particularly disturbed by a kid running for his life past them. A couple of women clutched their bags closer.

A dark tunnel yawned ahead of me.

I headed into it.

My breath was coming in shorter, harder gulps. I was almost at the end of my strength.

I turned to see where Red Singlet was.

I gasped in fright—he was almost on top of me! I could hear his panting, see the fury on his face, the rage in his narrowed eyes. He was going to make me pay for this chase. He could almost reach me. And my plan required that he did. I wasn't even sure that it would work, or how long before the tranquilliser would take effect.

I headed deeper into the gaping darkness of the tunnel, running along a siding that tapered ahead, narrowing until the platform finished at the tracks.

I had no choice—I jumped down and headed off into the tunnel, running as hard as I could along the tracks, where dim blue lights along the wall lit my way, and past the dark recesses of the human-sized safety alcoves at intervals along the tunnel.

I heard him jump down behind me with a grunt. And at that sound, I pulled off the lid of the syringe, and pretended to stumble on the tracks.

He roared with triumph and reared up, preparing to pounce on top of me.

I rolled over and held the syringe firmly pointed straight up but hidden out of sight.

He fell on me, grabbing me with his powerful hands, and I lunged upwards with the needle, jabbing him in the neck. I depressed the plunger before he had time to even realise what was happening.

He shrieked in pain and shock. Then loomed above me again, both his hands clenched, making a powerful martial arts-style weapon of his fists. He brought them down towards me and I barely had the strength to move out of his way.

His fists hit the edge of the left-hand rail first, and then his body followed, rolling over the track, the needle sticking out of his neck. I saw his eyes on me and the puzzled expression in them as he tried to get up, and fell back. He blinked, opened and closed his mouth, as if to speak. But no sound came out.

Then he crashed completely, his body flopped

out like a rag doll, his eyes rolled up into his head, and lay perfectly still.

'Sleep tight,' I whispered.

10:25 pm

I fell under a dim blue glow on the tunnel wall, my chest heaving. Every muscle ached and throbbed and I could feel blood dripping from the gash in the back of my leg. Some people back on the platform had started yelling and I knew it wouldn't be long before Security turned up. They'd find Red Singlet lying on the tracks inside the tunnel. They mustn't find me any-where near him.

I began picking my way along the tracks, scrambling over junction boxes and safety boxes running alongside the sleepers, when the rumblings of a train in another tunnel seemed to get louder.

At first I felt a cool breeze, and then there was a distinct rush of air coming towards me. The sound I could hear wasn't coming from a nearby tunnel—it was on *this* line. And it was speeding its way towards me!

Before running for the closest safety alcove, I stopped to look behind me at the lifeless shape of Red Singlet lying unconscious on the tracks. I hesitated, almost ignoring the urge to go back and move him, but couldn't . . . I just couldn't leave him in the path of an oncoming train.

The sound was almost unbearable as I hobbled back to Red Singlet's side. With all of my strength I pushed my hands underneath him, but as I began to heave his bulky body off the tracks the blue lights suddenly disappeared. Blackness fell heavily on my eyes and I panicked in the sudden darkness, and stumbled. Pain soared up my bad leg. The blue lights flickered and I saw that Red Singlet's body had rolled and tumbled off the tracks, but my blood-soaked foot had slipped between a sleeper and a safety box onto a metallic mesh ground . . . and become firmly wedged.

My foot was completely stuck.

The roar of the train was getting louder. I could now see its blazing lights in the distance behind me. Sweat rushed down my face as I desperately tried to free myself.

The sudden whoomp of pressured air hit my back as the train approached. Even more desperately, I tried to free myself, twisting this way then that, trying to wrench my foot out, trying to crawl off the tracks.

The train was bearing down on me. I could even see the cabin now, above the light. The driver had spotted me!

He'd applied the brakes and the train was screaming as he attempted to pull it up.

Would I lose my leg? Or my life?

I screamed but my voice was swallowed up by the terrible sound of the train's approaching wheels sparking against the brakes. Blazing lights blinded me; I was deafened by the screeching and the blaring horns echoing throughout the tunnel as the train thundered towards me. Frenzied, I struggled to free my trapped ankle! Straining every muscle of my body, I screamed for help!

The train would never pull up in time and I'd be creamed, minced on the tracks! I gave a last desperate heave, trying to escape. But my foot, trapped in the boot I'd taken from the zoo, wouldn't budge.

In slow motion, I watched the train come closer, my body frozen in horror. Time seemed to stop.

CONSPIRACY 365

BOOK THREE: MARCH

'I'm going crazy here, not knowing what the hell to do each day. I'll do anything that's going to get me and my family out of this hell-hole. You tell me, Boges — you're the smart one — why is all this happening? To me and my family? What am I supposed to do?'

Cal is drawing closer to the truth behind the Ormond Singularity, but now he's in more danger than ever. He's stolen vital information, and the thugs who are chasing him will stop at nothing to get it back. Can he make sense of the Ormond Riddle before they catch up with him?